THE COMET

AND OTHER STORIES

THE COMET

AND OTHER STORIES

SONYA MOOR

First published in the UK in 2023 by Confingo Publishing

249 Burton Road, Didsbury, Manchester M20 2WA

www.confingopublishing.uk

Copyright © Sonya Moor 2023
Sonya Moor has asserted her right to be identified as the author of this Work in
accordance with the Copyright, Designs and Patents Act 1988

Cover photographs by Christophe Dellière

Cover design by Zoë McLean

Typesetting by John Oakey

Printed by TJ Books Limited

A CIP catalogue record for this book is available from the British Library

ISBN 978-1-7393745-0-1

2 4 6 8 10 9 7 5 3 1

To P.V. Wolseley
for the love, loss and reasons to write

CONTENTS

Ekphrasis

Though now most often associated with poetry about art or, in prose, with art historical texts, ekphrasis originated in Classical rhetoric, where it took the form of descriptions so vivid they might be 'seen': words forged shields and painted frescoes, or brought to life people and places in the listener's mind's eye. The stories collected here are ekphrases in a broad sense; they pertain to art more generally, from visual and musical, to comedic and criminal. Some relate to works that disquieted or troubled, even enraged. Others to works that delighted, elated, or inspired. Put another way, they relate to works that 'spoke' to me. These stories attempt a response.

Sonya Moor
Paris, 2022

Lapin à la Moutarde

This early in the day, September feels like spring – with the blue still waking in the sky, and the air hazy with bristle fibres from the plane trees. It could almost be pollen or confetti. The sideboard looks ready for something wonderful to happen, with the olive oil standing to attention and those festive sprigs of parsley. Chirac is droning softly through the radio speakers, gracing the kitchen with a presidential address. Then – and isn't this just perfect? – his voice makes way for the march from *Marriage of Figaro*. All tippy toes and dancing skips. I wipe my hands on my apron, fling open the kitchen window wide to share the music with the birds.

Now back to the rabbit's fridge-chilled flesh. So cool against the skin. So soothing for hands still sore from bathroom cleaning – a perfect balm for my bleach burns.

Preparing a welcome meal is not without its pleasures. And a welcome meal for *three*! When Pascal said he was bringing his new girlfriend for lunch, it took all my self-discipline not to set the table there and then. I almost blurted, 'High time!' After all, it's too late to make poor Gérard proud and I'm getting no younger, not to mention Pascal himself. But I kept it all between me and the kitchen walls. 'Give him space,' I told myself, since Gérard is no longer here to remind me, bless his soul.

11

'Leftovers will do nicely,' is what Gérard would have said to all this fuss.

True, the freezer is still full from Pascal's last aborted visit. But I want this lunch to be just perfect. That's what I'd say, if Gérard were here to listen.

I've a good feeling about Pascal's new girl – something tells me she's a keeper. And there's poetry to Pascal having kept quiet about her these past few months. After all, he was *my* secret for the first twelve weeks of his life. My little treasure, buried safe. Not shared even with Gérard, because I knew by then that to tell Gérard was to tell Belle-mère.

I take a cleaver to the joints.

The rabbit bones crack like my knees.

My fingers gouge mustard from the pot and I daub the pink flesh yellow.

With these knuckles beginning to swell, these purple veins worming beneath the skin, I hardly recognise my hands any more. I could almost believe I was watching Maman working, working…

Where did they go, my lovely smooth-skinned hands?

And the rest?

For the table, I'll seat Pascal on my left and his girl on my right – pride of place. I'll dress the table with my wedding linens, white on white. Silver plate, not steel. Crystal, not glass. I'll do better than Belle-mère did by me – I'll treat this girl no less than if she were my own new-found daughter.

If she's the right sort.

I might teach her to make *lapin à la moutarde*, just like Maman taught me.

Well, not *exactly* like Maman taught. There'll be no hauling the rabbit from its pen to hang it head down. No bar to the back of the neck and a bucket of blood. No skinning – one swift tug, like shaking out a sheet. Certainly no sun-drying pelt.

Belle-mère wasted no time teaching me better.

There I was for 'tea', done up in my new collar – as much like marriage material as Maman could make me, by stitching in the mean hours after the day's cleaning jobs. Belle-mère – would-be mother-in-law, then – gave me one look and said, 'Is that *rabbit* fur?' I looked down to hide my blushes. She said no more, as if the shame were so great that was the kindest thing she could do for me.

Scalding it was.

I felt for all the world like these fat rabbit thighs, frying in oil so hot it spits.

After the wedding, Gérard gave me a magnificent beaver stole, all the way from Québec.

'Stunning!' he said, when I tried it on. If I'd managed to catch his eye with a wardrobe of two handmade dresses, I suppose I must have looked quite something in beaver. But I never could wear it.

'I keep thinking of the cost,' I told him.

'You needn't worry,' he said. 'It's Maman's treat.'

To be fair, Gérard made sure I never did have to worry – not about money, at least – but he managed to put his silly, well-meaning finger on the very thing that *was* troubling me. My thoughts had turned to Switzerland – to how costly a gift can be, for the receiver.

I said nothing, though.

We never did speak of Switzerland.

I'll chop the carrots good and fine.

It's a pleasure to be preparing them as seasoning, rather than main; these veg are all the last girl could have eaten. I'm glad things didn't work out for her and Pascal – between me and the kitchen walls, I can say so. She wasn't the sort for *lapin à la moutarde*. Always pursing her lips in silent judgement, pale eyes peering up from her computer-thing. She was too good for much, with all that learning. Hands so fine it was hard to imagine her wiping her bum, let alone making a bed. Much like Belle-mère. And all for giving me lessons. That time I offered her a blouse, she laid one finger on the fabric and pulled back as if burned. Thinking of Belle-mère offloading cast-offs, I said, 'It's new – just not my size.'

'I wear only natural fibres against my skin,' she said. There I was again. Cheeks blotched with shame. A rabbit-fur collar. Rabbit thighs in hot oil.

This new girl, whatever she's like, is another chance.

If she could be like the very first girl Pascal brought home, wouldn't that be wonderful? He had simpler tastes then – such a sweet, homely girl. Her name's lost to me, but I have a photo – stashed at the back and bottom of my purse. Behind receipts, bank cards. There! Still crumpled from when I saved her from Pascal's waste-paper basket. Dark eyes, sun-browned skin, a gentle smile. It seemed terribly wrong to throw her away.

If I'd had a girl, she might have looked like that.

Chantal, I'd have called her…

I'll prop her on the side while I work, like company, and have her gone before Pascal gets here.

There's the rabbit nicely browned.

I bundle it cleanly away beneath an upturned plate, ready for the next step, feeling none of the usual satisfaction – only a sharp little pang. I've begun to feel the burden of things put away, recently. It's as if the attic had started to groan under its load. Even small things weigh heavy. Like how to skin a rabbit – knowledge passed from Mamie, to Maman, to me, then mentioned no more after marriage. That knowledge will be lost, unless I pass it on in turn.

If Pascal's girl is the sort, I'll tell her how Maman gave the rabbit's innards to the dog, but saved the liver – you get a nice big liver on a rabbit. I'll tell her rabbit fur is quite decent, if you harvest it right – soft and warm.

Just the thing for baby boots...

Time to put the white wine on to simmer. The glug of it being poured into the pan always feels like a celebration.

But as the heat rises through, the smell rather catches the throat. There's something sinister about those golden heat-glimmers snaking their way up through the liquid. Strings of tiny bubbles streaming to the surface, rushing to escape. In my mind the pan melts, remoulds as glass. The wine becomes warm champagne, and once again I'm on my way to Switzerland.

I can almost hear Gérard's sister Suzette laughing with glee.

Little wonder. What a jaunt! We had bubbles and first-class tickets, thanks to Belle-mère.

'Think of it as a holiday,' Belle-mère had said, and I was determined to do so – or not to think at all, since thinking could do little good by that point. It was strange, at first, to be travelling with Suzette. She was more envoy than companion, I suppose – guard-cum-guide. We barely knew each other when we set off, but champagne broke the ice, and we were soon thick as thieves. Two runaways.

As we left Avignon, Provence chugged past, with its white crags and poplars jutting into the sky, and the olive trees cowering beneath the mistral. We couldn't leave fast enough for our liking, so we closed the curtains and then it was just us, blood-orange light filtering through the scrim, and dust motes dancing to the rhythm of the train. I felt lightheaded before I'd had even a drop to drink. Everything seemed possible. With one tug we'd blocked out the bold blue skies, the sledgehammer sun, and the stone-melting mistral. For the first time, I was leaving the place I'd been born and raised. Leaving home. No more scraping the bottom of every jar, no more putting aside peelings for soup, no more cutting up every small thing into smaller and smaller pieces so it would go round. I was done coming second to my brother, done handing over wages to poor Maman.

L'échappée belle!

'When you come back, everything will be different,' said Suzette, producing Gauloises to go with the bubbles. 'You and Gérard can do things properly, with a ring, a fairy-tale dress on the big day... You could have a billowing skirt and a cinch-waist like Grace Kelly. You'll be perfect, all in white.'

We drank and smoked as if it were already time to celebrate.

The bubbles in our cups kept rising, rising, each one like a promise of more.

Suzette showed me illustrations in a guidebook: mounts and meadows, the steep rise and fall of the land softened by a fuzz of grasses and wildflowers. Belle-mère had packed guidebooks in case of trouble at the border, but looking at those pictures, I was every bit the tourist. It wasn't just Switzerland I was setting out to discover, either – it was a whole new life.

I add the chopped carrots to the wine, plop in a plump garlic bulb, and watch them swirl and churn.

I'm not sure I moved with much more volition back then.

I was terribly young, really.

If life had been less harsh to start with, things might have been different. Belle-mère's talk about pain today for the sake of tomorrow made sense – little different from when we fled the bombings so fast we had to leave the dog. Or when I'd pick out a favourite kitten, knowing that before I got home from school Maman would have turned the rest into limp little bodies, like odd socks still wet from the wash. These days, I often spare a thought for the poor mother cat, prowling and yowling for her lost young, tail whipping the air in fury…

I take a blade to the parsley, and feel better for lopping off its hairy green head.

What is certain is that if Belle-mère hadn't been such a *salope* – I can say that too, to the kitchen walls – and with Gérard gone, God rest him – yes, if she hadn't been such a *véritable salope*, Switzerland would never have happened.

When Belle-mère summoned me for 'tea', I was all best behaviour, hoping only for wedding bells. Coming in from the street through those ancient carriage doors, I felt so small. So vulnerable, walking the length of that endless garden path, with its yews and palms lined up like a regiment. I hardly dared press down my heels for fear of messing the raked gravel. At the door, I gave the bell the slightest tug, but still it seemed to echo forever round the many rooms inside before at last opening.

There was Gérard, smiling.

The sight of him was never such a pleasure as then – not even on our wedding day. He was tall, sure. So cultivated in his suit and tie. He took my hand as if I were already his lady-wife and led me inside. Once in the soothing coolness of their entrance hall, standing before the great sweep of staircase, which coiled up three floors at least, I dared believe for the first time in weeks that everything would be fine.

Then Gérard took me in to Belle-mère.

That thought gets my mezzaluna going; I'll make short work of this parsley.

'Poor child!' she said. 'Having to ring like a tradesman! I *specifically* asked for someone to accompany you.' Her apologies left me feeling at fault for an unspecified *faux pas*. I looked to Gérard for guidance, but he had gone; in his place was a boy in Sunday best, looking at his mother as if to ask, 'Is my tie straight? Would you straighten it?'

Belle-mère gave a nod to Gérard, and to me said, 'Please, dear, do sit.'

Gérard led me to a high-backed armchair that left me hemmed in on all sides. He muttered something about us ladies getting better acquainted; his voice strained as if he'd erred into a women's powder room.

And he left.

I must watch myself with the mezzaluna. The blade's a blur.

What *was* he thinking? That mother knew best? That it was *une affaire de femmes*?

Now he's gone, I'll never know.

But I do know this: even when he left me for the great ever-after, I never felt so abandoned as I did that day.

Et voilà: parsley chopped fine as angel's breath.

Belle-mère offered me tea and Harlequin-coloured financiers. She made small talk that somehow sounded grand – great decorous airy sentences that lifted and fluttered like the gauzy curtains at the windows to their garden. It was all so lovely – too lovely. Every 'please' and 'thank you', every delicious bite, every sip from the dainty gold-trimmed cup in my hand left me feeling exposed, as if I was chalking up some mysterious bill; some immense, unpayable debt.

'Gérard explained to me your "delicate situation",' she said eventually.

I looked into my cup, examined the pale brown liquid, the white glow of porcelain beneath.

'More tea?' she said.

I make a start on the shallots, slicing precise, premeditated cuts, still wholeheartedly hating her for that delay.

'*Merci*,' was all I could say. I wanted Maman and her rough ways. It had never occurred to me before then that it was pure kindness, the way she put the rabbits out of their misery so swiftly.

'Gérard intends to do the honourable thing,' said Belle-mère. 'I can count on you to do likewise?'

I thought she meant marriage. Like a fool, I gave a determined nod.

Belle-mère brightened. She spoke about how lucky I was ('A family like ours… a girl like you…'). How she herself had come up in the world by marrying well. How Gérard would provide properly for his family, now that he had been offered such a promising position as director of the family allocations office.

'I'll make a director's wife of you yet,' she said.

My collar tightened.

Still, it was only when she said, 'Gérard's credibility in his new position would be entirely undermined by any unseemly rush up the aisle,' that the blood drained from my head.

She spoke of 'solutions'. My mind swirled with all the whispered horror stories I'd ever heard: kitchen-table angel makers, knitting needles, rusted iron wires… The room tilted. I put down my cup for fear of spilling it.

My eyes smart now as they did that day. If anyone were here to see, I'd blame the shallots.

Belle-mère noticed, back then.

Perhaps she feared I'd refuse to cooperate? She was certainly quick to clarify: 'I would feel uncomfortable sending you anywhere other than Switzerland.' She spoke of specialised clinics where the paperwork could be sorted in advance, told me I needn't worry about the cost – she'd consider it part of the wedding expenses. 'You would be accompanied, of course,' she said. 'Suzette will be there for you.'

The tears came properly then. Perhaps partly from relief that I would be spared a visit to some backstreet kitchen-butchery. Belle-mère's own eyes were red-rimmed, as if the 'solution' was something we had worked out together. Still, when she handed me her handkerchief, I hesitated; it was such a perfect square of pure white cotton, hemmed by tiny stitches and decorated with a fine Calais-lace panel – too beautiful to soil. But when I looked again at those edges, rolled tight and neat as a new leaf, I reached out and took it.

'There, there,' said Belle-mère. Though I hated her for speaking more softly than Maman ever did, my heart was heavy with thankfulness.

I kept that handkerchief; it seemed understood that I would. It is folded away and so carefully laundered, it looks unused, pristine.

I fry the shallots gently, to keep them sweet.

Add bay leaf to the white wine.

More thyme too, I think.

Think...

I didn't, at the time. At least, I tried my hardest not to.

It seems almost grotesque now: Suzette and I giggled and chatted nearly all the way to Switzerland. I suppose we were getting through as best we could.

As we neared the border, Suzette uncovered the windows. 'For the view,' she said. I feared that she was scene-setting – making clear that we had nothing to hide. With the sudden sun in my face, I felt like I'd been pushed onstage, into the spotlight. Or worse, like I'd been shoved into place for an interrogation.

Suzette squeezed my hand.

'We'll have no awkward questions,' she said. 'I know from last time.'

It took me a moment to find the full meaning of her words.

She gazed out the window, raised a hand to her necklace, lifted the pearls from her collar bone. I remembered her boss's generosity paying for her previous Swiss 'holiday'. And the necklace – a gift once she was back behind her typewriter. I understood why she'd been elected as my companion. It came not so much in a flash as on a wave of nausea.

A weighty silence settled between us.

My mind swarmed, suppressed worries rising like the streaming armies of ants in Maman's kitchen. I was on the brink of choking out, 'I'm not sure about this.' But Suzette spoke first, filling the awkward silence as people so often do, with that little joke about an angel passing: '*Un ange passe!*'

She refilled my cup though it wasn't empty, and proposed a toast: 'Here's to better to come!'

When we arrived, it did seem that there might be better days ahead. Everything at the clinic was so new and white, so bright and clean. Like a smart hotel – at least, like the smart hotels I had imagined. There were nurses everywhere asking, 'Is Madame comfortable? Shall I get you anything?' It seemed too late to reply other than with a smile and a shake of the head.

I add the rabbit to the shallots, pour in the white wine mixture.
Almost done.

Into the oven it goes, to cook properly: long and slow. *Securely lidded.*

I felt much the same when I woke at the clinic: hospital corners held the sheets in place so firmly, I was all but bound to the bed. And still those gentle voices asked, 'Is Madame comfortable? Can I get anything for Madame?' If I could have, I'd have asked for everything to be undone. But I fell asleep again, and dreamt of wedding robes, and funeral shrouds, and my future mother-in-law tucking me in too tight.

*

- Hello, my *chou*. What time will you be in?

- Ah? Not the high-speed train? If you check, you might still be able to get a quicker train from Nîmes. I made your favourite.

- *Lapin à la moutarde*, of course! It should be ready by one-thirty.

- I see. Well, you and I could eat the rabbit, and I could prepare a salad for... Katy. Katy? She's not French then?

- That's a bit much, darling. I'm sure she'll understand that, here, rabbit is no different from any other meat. She might be curious to discover regional cooking.

- Well, yes. In that case, I can see it might seem *like* offering stewed dog or cat. Still, a farmed rabbit is not the same as a pet.

- No, no, I *do* see. I'll put it away for another day. Another time.

- When will you be in?

- There's plenty to see and do right here. Katy might like to see Avignon Bridge, the Pope's palace...

- No that's fine. Nîmes is lovely, it's true.

- No, it's fine. Next week is fine. Really.

*

With the sky clouded over, the fibres from the plane trees look less like confetti – more like the dried flowers the undertakers gave out at Gérard's funeral to scatter on his grave. And with the warmth gone out of the day, that's a cruel mistral.

As I shut the window, the wind blasts in for a last swagger round the kitchen, rifling papers, picking up and dropping the photo of that dear girl. There's no panic to tidy her away, now that Pascal's not coming. I reach out to prop the picture up again, but my hand falters. I settle for letting the picture lie flat on the sideboard, thinking to get on with the next steps of the recipe – the cream, the lemon juice... But it seems so stupid, futile, to fill an already full freezer.

Another option: I could do away with the whole damn lot.

Let the wind take the photo.

Throw away the meal.

But I feel that curious lightness I first felt in Switzerland, like I've been cored – a small, deep emptiness. I'm bored right through with it. I lower myself into a chair, its legs and mine creaking in protest. I take a breath in, a breath out. And I sit. Listening to the rabbit simmering, for a child that won't come.

A Steal

From: victoria.ellis@libertysurf.fr
To: amandajanewilloughby@hotmail.com
Date: 01/03/15 at 15:05
Re: Get glass of something – long email

Mands,

You know how you joke that I do household accounting for fun, like most people do gardening? Well, is not funny any more: garden has been broken into. Am telling you first-ish, as BFF. Sat down with spreadsheet spic and span – debits and credits lined up nicely. Spent some time wondering if bits might grow better if moved to diff. account or if more exposed to risk etc., then for maxi fun (not funny) went online to reconcile own records with bank statement. Did usual padlocked-portal-personal-code palaver to enter my space, got ready for total satisfaction of seeing bank balance as expected to the last cent, and found: mess. Couldn't recognise own account. Massive debits strewn all over – cheque numbers from chequebook due by post but never delivered. Blood – that's what I thought I saw. Also thought it might be mine, as heart was pumping hard enough to spring a leak. But no – was not blood. Was balance: so heavily in red, was like scene from Tarantino movie.

Pierre came to the rescue with hotline (P = crap with most practical stuff, but amazing in emergency). I keyed in nos., imagining superhero hit squad powering up at other end, got myself all mother's-maiden-name ready, then got through to a robot. Options: 'cancel card' or 'cancel cheque'. No 'declare heinous crime'. No 'summon justice'. Pressed '2', and had to say postcode. Get this: voice could not be recognised. P took the phone and said postcode – didn't enunciate or anything. '*C'est ton accent*,' he said, as if that somehow made OK a world in which voice recognition thingy can give shit service.

Eventually got through to the Banque de France and discovered is not enough to say 'chequebook stolen and bank account haemorrhaging'. Word is not enough. Must write them a letter. And even that not enough. Must get letter stamped by bank, go to police, and make statement; only then can cancel cheques. Believe? So wrote letter – the sort that estranges self from self: 'I wish to cancel the following cheques…', as if was dearest desire. Stating nos. 'from… to, inclusive' was my only comfort – the only indication that I'm me, and that money garden is truly mine.

Soz for whinge. Thnx so much for listening. The lovely P has brought glass of red – will help. Hope you're having one too.

Big kiss – both cheeks,

V.

*

From: victoria.ellis@libertysurf.fr
To: amandajanewilloughby@hotmail.com
Date: 02/03/15 at 19:23
Re: Re: Re: Get glass of something – long email

Mands, had nightmare making police statement! Presented self to be registered and woman at desk asked for nature of complaint and ID, so she could take name. I asked how come, when queuing system is numbered. Was told names and nature of complaint are taken so numbered queue can be interrupted with urgent cases. I explained how case is urgent. Woman at desk said is not urgent, as no blood spilt. My number: 133.

After an eternity, no. comes up but woman at desk calls P's surname, not mine, so I go to desk and explain how I use maiden name. Policeman charged with taking statement chips in: 'But you are married?' as if was his business. I say yes, but use maiden name, coz is 2015 and feminism has happened, and is my right. He waves me forward saying, '*Encore une…*' – 'Another one…' One what?! Believe the cheek?

I got ready to remind him: me public, you public servant = you my servant, but he took me to small cell-like room so grim was gobsmacked: table nailed to floor, chairs all splay-legged, walls covered in some wipe-clean stuff that had been wiped, but not clean, so dirt slalomed all over. Seemed not v. appropriate to explain how policeman is servant, as could not explain working conditions. It's weird, as taxes = super high; where does money go?

Asked how long will take to catch fraudster. Policeman said can take months, coz lack of resources. Could not believe, but then became eyewitness to world's slowest policeman typing statement with one finger, on computer dating from Cretaceous. Had nothing to do but meditate on badly drawn penis graffiti on back of computer.

Was asked to read statement before signing. Found had used words would never use in real life, like 'usurpation' and 'perpetrator'. Discovered policeman's name is Monsieur Vincent Leroy, guardian of the peace. Couldn't resist pointing out spelling errors, as is too delicious for *un rosbif* to correct a Frog's

French, but Vincent Leroy looked uncomfortable. Found self sorry for him – noticed how he was big man made for action, dressed in silly cheap suit – fabric like disposable napkin. Knees hardly fitted under desk. Unseemly. So left some dodgy spelling, but insisted on all numbers being correct. Vincent Leroy executed order as if was empty exercise, which made me uneasy. To remind him job = catching crim, I asked technical question: how is fraudster using cheques, given that in France you need ID for cheque payments? Got shrug and goodbye. Am not sure I exist in eyes of state.

Got home super tense. First instinct was to go to money garden to relax, but the joy's gone. Fraudster has stolen that too.

Promise this is last whingey email I'll send. So grateful for stress release.

All OK your end?

Bigguns,

V.

*

From: victoria.ellis@libertysurf.fr
To: amandajanewilloughby@nationaltrust.org.uk
Date: 16/03/15 at 09:17
Re: Exclusive invitation

Mands, so sorry, but won't be able to make your signing. Jolly jaunt to London out of question, as am drowning in claims from creditors threatening legal proceedings if cannot prove cheques were stolen. At first was pleased to get post – got that feeling of something special just for me (remember licked envelopes and SWALKs?). Have now developed fear of white envelopes. P says mustn't take it personally, but in what world is post not personal? P says not to bother even reading, just collect claims to give to police, but am too much the citizen; cannot ignore carefully typed correspondence.

Fraudster has spent fortune at H&M. Weird place to splurge. Would love to know what she bought. Maybe a new look, to go with new persona? But then why not go somewhere decent? She also spent 52.90 EUR at Flunch. Who lunches at Flunch?! She's been spending big and often at Monoprix supermarket – once at my local branch. Would love to know what she's putting in trolley. How come so expensive? Does she buy only organic?

Is super weird to think we might have met. There's a guy sells charity newspapers at the door. I never buy (don't do charity unless can get receipt for tax deduction – is best to give responsibly). I do give smile though, because the guy always says, '*Bonjour, ma belle.*' Did he say that to the other 'Victoria'? Did she buy his newspaper? If so, would that in any way reflect on me? Would it make me a better or worse person?

Have started getting junk mail from shops where 'Victoria' spent my cheques; bad-debtor post at same time as valued-customer post. Feel as if self is splitting and multiplying. Have received so much marketing from one store, think she must have put me on mailing list. Is a furniture store – all ethnic fabrics, rattan tables… Hideous. If that's her idea of gorgeousness, why would she sign up for mailing list, knowing that post would go to me? Where's the logic? Or was it more about dreams and desires? Was she wanting to live dream? To live it, for as long as it took to give my name and address – to be 'Victoria' even if only in imagination of shop assistant signing 'me' up? I flick through the catalogue and wonder if I'm wandering through her dreamscape – if we might meet in this imaginary space. Might I be looking at a mega-yuk wickerwork chair thinking 'who would buy that?' while she's running an imaginary finger along the armrest thinking 'I wish…'?

Soz, soz, soz not to be with you Saturday. Can't believe I'll be graffiti-penis gazing at police station, instead of supporting BFF's book launch. Will be with you in spirit. XOXO

*

From: victoria.ellis@libertysurf.fr
To: amandajanewilloughby@hotmail.com
Date: 07/04/15 at 10:30
Re: Thanks and praise for monograph!

Mands,

Am awed! Hope National Trust knows how lucky they are to have you on staff – you've singlehandedly put Spencer back on culture map. Sensible to send book by super-security sign-for post – even if, as you say, art books are sadly less vulnerable to theft than chequebooks. Felt self-conscious signing. Wondered how other 'Victoria' signs. Swankily? With flourish?

Just got back from spending more quality time with Monsieur Vincent Leroy, guardian of the peace, and his graffiti penis – now see it on the back of my eyelids. 'Victoria' has opened mobile-phone lines with direct debits on my account. Got letter from Liberté Télécom welcoming me as new customer and offering deal for those with family and friends in North Africa (only person I know from North Africa is cleaning lady). Also found out that I have committed two offences on public transport – was invited to pay without delay the fine imposed as a result of my antisocial behaviour.

On upside, Vincent Leroy said police would now take case seriously (felt like crying but managed smile). Asked how long before fraudster stopped? He said best close bank account, as these things take time. Pointed out: 'Victoria' is steadily work-

ing through chequebook; even I can reconstruct her move-
ments from claimants' letters; and we could trace her on one of
her mobile-phone numbers. So maybe Sherlock not needed?

Monsieur Leroy said is not Sherlock needed – is resources.
Said police actually v. reactive when danger of physical harm.
So said: am harmed. Am being harassed by creditors; might
be pursued for non-payment of fine. Said: world cannot be the
domain of a privileged few who go through life immune to the
consequences of their acts. Said: is unfair that I pay for someone else's crime. Said: do I need lawyer to get justice?

Leroy shifted in seat – think is sensitive to the justice thing.
Said he'd do what he could to get public transport authority
off back, so rang to get info on fines – had to use my mobile,
as police phones not authorised to dial 0800 – believe? Found
out that 'Victoria' has *two* IDs in my name. Birth date would
make her ten years younger than me, which is what my expensive face cream offers – feel that once again, she's got what I'm
paying for. My man Vincent ran search on ID, confirmed they
were fake, told Public Transport as much. They said, 'We need
it in writing.' Vincent exasperated. Quite a bonding experience.

Making statement went pretty fast. Know deal now. Time
for chat at end with Vince. Says Victoria got ID sorted so fast,
chequebook might have been stolen to order. Says is pro job.
Felt flattered: if must be scammed, prefer high-quality crim.

Lots,

V.

*

From: victoria.ellis@libertysurf.fr
To: amandajanewilloughby@hotmail.com
Date: 13/04/15 at 21:59
Re: Re: Do this

Darling, thank you for Proust questionnaire. Is excellent idea to get self down on paper – am sure will help sort out head. Need it more than ever. Saw the question 'your chief characteristic' and thought 'independence'. Me, right? But then thought, how independent am I given that 'Victoria' has stolen name, time, and money? For question on greatest unhappiness, would be losing everything: money, job, flat, family, friends, BFF – you, Pierre, name, body, mind... How much can be stripped away before there's no more 'me'?

During lunchbreak shopping, tried on clean-lined shift dress and investment-buy wrap dress, and caught sight of this pitiful pink-skinned creature in changing-room mirror. There was so little to distinguish shrimpy naked self from any other human, I had to avert my gaze. Thought, with a shudder, of hymn that used to give us giggles in school assembly: 'I was cold, I was naked, were you there?' Thought of humans with less, humans with nothing, and found self on sort of mental border, unable to go beyond – too afraid that I might get thrown out of my own life forever.

Oh dear – actually, will wait till feeling more like self before tackling Proust questionnaire...

Soz, Mands. Know am being maudlin. Think it's coz have appointment tomoz for closure of bank account. Am abandoning garden. I know account no., BIC, IBAN, access codes, etc. by heart. After closure, will have keys to a place that no longer exists. Sniff.

Massive ones,

V.

*

Today, 10:05, me:
Sorted! New account better than old! Manager super-understanding as suffered ID fraud himself. Mega deal on international transactions so money garden can extend easily across borders. Feel fully myself. Will tackle Proust ques.! Xxxx

*

From: victoria.ellis@overy.com
To: amandajanewilloughby@hotmail.com
Date: 21/04/15 at 10:35
Re: Crim to be clinked?

Mands, newsflash: bank manager rang to say someone went into branch in Sevran (had never heard of it – P says is ghetto suburb) and tried to cash one of my cheques. Bank has CCTV footage, so have 'Victoria' on film! Of course, I went to bank manager and asked what she looked like. Bank manager couldn't say – legal reasons – but described her as *racaille* ('lowlife'). Was disappointed that fraudster is not the glam 'executive crim' I'd imagined – felt like a personal slight – then pricked up ears because bank manager was saying, '*Je ne suis pas raciste, mais…*' but stopped.

I deduced that 'Victoria' must be non-white. Bank manager's half-sentence kept coming at me like emotional reverb. Felt chill, as if suddenly outside own skin. Was shaken back into it by bank manager giving energetic handshake, and telling me that scales of justice are shifting. Left wobble-legged and less sure than should be of what this means.

Xo

*

From: victoria.ellis@libertysurf.fr
To: amandajanewilloughby@hotmail.com
Date: 21/04/15 at 23:59
Re: Can't sleep

Mands, a naughty late night one – may I? P sleeping but not me – can't. Know you turn off devices, so won't disturb…

Have swank bank account, enough police statements to paper-bomb anyone giving me admin grief, and crim is surely as good as caught, so should be laughing, but 'Victoria' = still taking up mind-space. Keep wondering who she is. Maybe need her identity, as is what she stole from me? Or need to figure her identity in order to get back mine? To retrace the borders?

Did silly thing: typed 'Sevran' into search engine – way stalkerish. Should have felt weirder than it did. Results: rural-idyll district names (Rougemont, Beaudottes…), urban-hell headlines ('local school in radicalisation row', 'dead man found face down dressed as superhero', 'kid's killer condemned'), and stats (population quadrupled in forty years, 30% immigrants, 36% below the poverty line…).

Went walkabout with Street View: found self in car park pitted with potholes as if was war zone. To the left: a sapling that had given up before it had started. Right: a pram-pushing female with face blurred to oblivion. Ahead: an abandoned shopping trolley. Above: blue, blue sky – the right sort for picturesque central Paris – for streets where sun can appropriately shine. There, it seemed to add insult to injury.

Back on the search results page, saw links to a music video and thought, 'Salvation! Sevran has art!' So I clicked. A rapper swaggered on to screen. Voice thick with the accent of the ghetto suburbs – sounds rolled in back of nose and throat, then spat out. No pretty pursed-lipped sounds of standard French.

A cave-dweller's voice – throttled, angry.

I cut sound. Just watched. A pit bull. Something burning in a barrel. A trashed car trampled by a huddle of hooded figures. Then a new shot: two women in strips of ill-fitting, elasticated lace, served up on a tabletop, like someone's lunch. One woman moves towards rapper guy, and camera drops to her bum as she does a jelly-jiggle. I feel strongly the need to look her in the eye – see what she's feeling – but camera leers over her teeming dimples.

Now a bathroom scene. A woman in a mini dress. Rapper guy gestures to the girl. She must strip. (This I understood – how? Is the language of aggression so universal?) Now the woman's in underwear. Rapper guy takes her by the neck, bends her over a bath, and she sticks her fingers down her throat. Being forced to make herself sick? Something to do with drug smuggling? Whatever the scene's about, it's clear that this woman can't lay claim to her stomach, and I feel sick – sick to the bottom of my own stomach.

I closed the window. Sevran black-holed into itself, but head was left completely trashed; a riot of rapper guys and pit bulls. So I opened email – wrote to you.

And here I am, still thinking, 'Is that where she's from? How could anyone live there?'

Thanks for listen. Love. V.

*

From: victoria.ellis@libertysurf.fr
To: amandajanewilloughby@hotmail.com
Date: 22/04/15 at 15:00
Re: Revolution now

Thanks for message, lovely. Yes, am all right, but P has booked me into therapy.

After monster email (soz – cheeks v. pink), still couldn't sleep. Returned to money garden, but Sevran tower blocks loomed in front, to the sides and behind, making carefully tended borders look silly – like topiary hedge around bunker.

Stared at screen so long got trippy. Found self wondering if French tendency to keep difficult elements segregated in suburbs is in any way related to the French tradition of tidy gardens. Also wondered how healthy this is: what if things are more connected than they – I – like to think? What if tidiness of my garden depends on keeping 'mess' out? What if 'mess' is people and places and lives?

Determined to pull self together. Left garden – was having no fun anyway – and went wandering around Web, looking for outings to divert self and lift spirits.

Stumbled upon outreach programme: charity called Ouverture – takes art to impoverished areas – gets kids making music, etc. Had revelation: am actually Lady Di/Gandhi. Epiphany! Felt like sun coming up (which it was, by that point). Set up permanent breach in garden boundary there and then, with monthly direct debit to Ouverture. Also dashed off thank-you note to Monsieur Vincent Leroy (selected Basquiat post-card – will be perfect juxtaposed with graffiti penis).

P woke to croissants and a charity newspaper from the guy outside Monoprix (turns out he's there from sun-up till sun-down). P ignored gifts, told me I looked *malade*. Seemed quite scared. I tried to reassure, by explaining how am done with being a victim – done with there being victims at all, anywhere in the world; am transforming all, by becoming the change I want to see.

P foot-stampingly cross. Made croissants jump by banging

hand on table. Said was being Marie-Antoinette-ish and didn't I see, this was exactly like the time I got sentimental over a sleeping homeless drunk and tried to fix all by slipping him twenty euros? As P fumed, he made coffee, lining up espressos like shots. After three, had to admit that revolution did look more 'token toe-dip' than 'storming of barricades'. So started to cry. P (darling chap!) held me to manly breast, while ringing doctor friend for recommended therapists.

Actually feel much better now, after sleep. If go through with sessions, any advice? Freud or Jung? Or are both old hat?

Oox

*

Today, 16:35, me:

Fraudster arrested! First thought: if she's sent down, will get closure. But police say fraudster was puppet, meaning juvenile used to do dirty business, as can't be jailed. Have been asked to meet her – scheme called Reconnect to help rehabilitation of crims by 'humanising' victims. Feel v. uncomfortable with idea that I need humanising – am not human enough already?! But need to know who she is, so have agreed. Am thinking might use your Proust questionnaire. Maybe if can get her down on paper will be able to get head in order, and could get closure that way – re-establish proper boundaries? Xo

*

From: victoria.ellis@libertysurf.fr
To: amandajanewilloughby@hotmail.com
Date: 01/06/15 at 15:05
Re: project Closure

M,

Status report on project Closure, as promised…

In short: got none.

Longer version: still trying to figure what happened, if anything.

Day started badly. Couldn't think what to wear to be 'humanised'. Opted for dressing down à la Princess Di landmine outfit. Arrived at appointment and realised would need to be in stained lino and gross-weave canvas in utility orange to fit with surroundings. Kissed off lipstick into tissue and stashed bracelet in bag.

Waiting room did nothing to ease nerves. Tried to mentally rehearse list of wrongs to be expressed, but guilt-inducing institutional environment kept inspiring questions like, 'How did I end up here? What did I do wrong?' Developed inverted imposter syndrome – worried that I didn't look sufficiently victim-like. Felt it showed that the only things I've ever failed are driving test and Pepsi challenge. Also got weird criminal-justice version of blind date nerves. Sat with hand on jittery stomach, silently asking, 'What if I don't recognise her? What will I say?'

Name was called after long wait. Was led to naked room like interrogation cell. There she was, placed facing door as if on display: a girl – she was barely more than that. Bad hair, frizzed as if after a fright. Eyes *farouche* – full of fear and fierceness. Twiglet limbs, which softened my heart, but girl's legs stuck out like a provocation and were kitted in urban-warfare joggers. On her feet: oversize trainers, tied with the tongues sticking out.

Overall impression: sweet like Chucky.

'Please sit,' said official-looking person, gesturing to chair. Not even a table between girl and me. Only protection was official person sat to side, like umpire. Pulled chair back as far as politely could before sitting.

While official person read terms-and-conditions thing, my heart and lungs were going like a cardio workout. Made super-human effort to sit composed and look like was listening, but since official person sat slumped and girl sat picking at sleeves, I couldn't think why I was taking pains. Official person said something about having to maintain the minor's anonymity. My gut was so parboiled by anger, I almost had to jump up to let out steam. Only thing that stopped me was a snort from the girl, who said, 'Yeah, right, that's what worries me. When my brother gets hold of me —'

Official person cut in. Reminded girl of seriousness of situation. Girl glowered into chest and pinched cuff hard as if punishing it.

It occurred to me that girl's 'puppet master' might be her own brother. Hypothesis made 'humanising' me shrink in importance next to issue of sorting out girl's home life. Even so, when official person interrupted my thoughts to ask me to introduce self, I wanted to refuse. Didn't want to give any more of self than had already been taken. Managed to dredge up only the corporate intro I use for roundtables at work.

Official person asked about effect of crime, but by this point, was wondering when girl would be asked to apologise. Did my best to talk of lost hours, admin and stress, but girl kept bothering her cuff. Felt blood rush. Said: 'You have no idea!'

Girl looked up. Gaze felt like punch.

'What idea do *you* have —' she said. Accent was so thick, her words came with a whiff of burning tyre.

Official person barked her down: 'You're here to listen.'

Felt moment's satisfaction, but then looked at girl — little head shrinking into a hoody, shoulders high and skinny like a broken hanger. I could still hear the rip in the air where her words should have been. Tried to mentally complete sentence, but couldn't – didn't know enough.

Your Proust questionnaire came to mind.

'I have a question,' I said to official person. She raised her eyebrow. Before she could yay or nay me, I asked girl about her heroes.

She looked up with a 'who me?' face, then shot a glance at official person, who tilted head in a half-nod.

'Not Nicki Minaj,' the girl said, belligerent. She gave the official person a sidelong look. No response. She eased into her subject: 'Not Nicki Minaj, with her airbags out all the time.'

Made me laugh out loud. The girl laughed too. She looked younger: a Tinkerbell light in each eye and a beautiful smile – all the more lovely for badly needing braces.

The girl looked down, suddenly shy. Plucked crossly at cuff, but carried on talking – said she liked Tinashe, and liked her name too. Said she wouldn't have chosen her own name, if she'd had a choice. '*Trop typé*,' she said.

It felt like an accusation. I rushed to say, 'There are some lovely Arabic names,' then wanted to gnaw off tongue, as sounded too like bank manager ('*je ne suis pas raciste…*'). Also worried she'd ask for examples – was set to give cleaning lady's, but got panic-induced mind-bug and couldn't remember it. So I said, 'I'm sure your name means something nice.'

'It means doing good,' she said.

'Like "virtuous"?' I said, to give free word-upgrade. I gift-wrapped it with a question mark, not to sound patronising.

Official person cut in, restated clause about maintaining anonymity.

The girl grew – doubled in size. Two-thirds of her became mouth, and all of it snarling. 'You tripping?' she said to the social worker person. 'You off your head?' She pointed to me.

I dodged instinctively, although it was only a finger she was pointing. 'Does she look like she speaks Arabic?' She turned to me, said, 'What the fuck would you do with my name anyway, when it's not worth shit?'

Felt nailed to chair by the force of her outburst. Worse, felt chair sink through floor, weighted by this thought: the girl had a point.

Official person repeated anonymity clause, voice now gritty and growling. Girl sank into shoulders again. I did likewise, not sure if was for fear or shame.

Rest of meeting passed in minimal questions and answers. I yesed and noed as quick as could, eager to go, as had written the whole thing off as a mess.

But when I stood to go at end of meeting, the girl stopped me: 'Eh, Madame.'

I felt the spirit of Gandhi/Lady Di flutter within, but heart was still on lockdown; giving anything of self seemed doable as ripping off own flesh to feed another human.

The girl floundered: 'Madame?' A pause. Then girl closed the meeting with a goodbye.

Get this though – she did it in English: 'Goudbaie.' Her face lit up again with that child's smile – cheeky and proud to have picked up on my accent. Don't know if there was any 'sorry' or 'thank you' there, but it felt real.

I so wanted, in that moment, to be able to call her by her name.

Settled for sharing weak smile and one word of my language: 'Goodbye.'

Was handed victim-support leaflets on way out, but felt a fraud taking them. Once in metro, dumped them in recycling.

Got home heavy-hearted. Looked out of kitchen at zinc-roof sea and pebble-beach-coloured buildings of Paris.

Picture-postcard view did nothing to stop me worrying about the girl, wondering was I human enough for her? Surely 'humanisation' should be a two-way thing? Shouldn't she at least have a name? Wanted to restore it to her. Googled: 'Arabic name means virtuous'. I found: Saliha.

So maybe that's it?

Whatever she's called, it seems to me now that her name's been stolen away and emptied of meaning – more surely than mine ever was.

X.

After Ever Happy

A thin gold band lies abandoned on a double bed.

The ring backflips, then springs into the forefinger and thumb of the young woman who set it there. She looks at it sidelong, as she might at something that must be shed – a bloodied plaster, splinter, or scab. Then she slips it on her ring finger, slowly, deliberately, unmaking a solemn commitment to herself. The ring constricts till it sits too tight at the base of her finger, and she fancies she can feel the inscription cutting into her skin three words: 'Happy ever after'.

She breathes in a sigh till her lungs are tight with tension, and frisks pockets and bag for things she knows are there: phone, bank card, keys to her mum's place. Outside, streetlamps snuff their sodium glow; it's time. She stands, the sheets smooth and the memory foam mattress forgets her. She is a ghost of her future self.

Her grip loosens and clothes fly from the mouth of her bag. Underwear flutters, a pair of jeans stretches its legs, a sweater flings wide its arms. She snatches the items from the air and flicks each one folded – so small and flat they slip into a single drawer, which she closes quietly.

She backs from bedroom to bathroom, each foot-rise

sending fear spiralling to the pit of her belly. She doesn't know, exactly, why she's holding her breath, but it's got something to do with control, with 'more haste, less speed', and with speed being of the essence.

As she drops her toothbrush into its polka-dotted cup, she gazes longer than she should at his 'n' hers, pink and blue, cosily coupled. She catches her eye in the mirror, engages herself in a stare down. Probing her reflection, she asks just *who* this clean-up is for, then daubs blood beneath her nose with a ball of damp cotton wool.

She slips a phone from her pocket as if it were stolen goods, hangs up, and holds the receiver whisper-close, one hand shielding the mouthpiece. Her eyes are on the door even though it's locked.

She gives hushed thanks in answer to her mother's voice – her mum's 'what-time-d'you-call-this-young-lady' tone – Mum trying so hard to make this conversation as safe as rushed homework, missed curfews, and other small perils from which she once emerged unscathed. Mum promises to pick her up – an abstract notion that floats somewhere above and beyond the reality of thumping heart, roaring pulse and ringing ears.

'Pop' – that's the wrong word: too casual, for this time of night. The woman tests her swollen lip with a tooth, gauging pressure. A silence bulges, stretched by a mother's contained fear. The woman says she's popping round. She speed-dials her mum.

Halfway down the stairs, backing from bathroom to kitchen, she knows what she must do. Her plan unhatches as she descends, one foot behind the other, till it's nothing but a small hard-shelled egg of certainty buried beneath her solar plexus. In the kitchen, her knees buckle beneath her as she backslides down the wall to the floor. She sits in brace position, forehead to kneecaps, for she doesn't know how long.

There's a terrible silence thickening and swelling. The sort of silence that must have existed before *om* or whatever word was the beginning. The silence that might set in the day the sky turns black and those famous horsemen finally appear. A soupy, churning silence, full of something about to happen.

It starts with a slam. A door is flung open so fast and hard, the backdraft is slurped into a vacuum. Her lover – she doesn't yet think that's the wrong word – hurtles, back first, into the room and posts himself by the pedal bin. His arm and leg pull back, as if reeled in by a greater power. His right boot jerks from the bin with a bang, and the dent in its drum is swallowed into a sudden and perfect cylinder.

She's not sure how – it happens so fast – but then he's in her face, snorting air, yelling how he never laid a finger – not once, not once: so many imploding word-blasts that leave her eardrums intact.

A hush rises. He stares as if stunned – as if he has no idea why they are standing so close – as if he has never seen her before in his life. The red sluices from his face, flushed by a wash of white. In words so soft he might be trying to convince himself, he swears he would *never* touch her. His pupils ping big as a trickle of blood creeps up her lip to her nose.

She knows the blood is coming. She gets nosebleeds – though it's usually hot weather or a sneeze that sets them off, not panic. The ebb tide of blood to a sting behind her septum feels portentous, revelatory – like her body's own strange confirmation of another bloodletting that she now knows must come, one way or another, even if it's by her own hand. A random thought occurs: never again will she wonder why mother hamsters, when afraid, murder their young.

Cups in the cupboard quake as her wrist is wrenched from the wall into the manacle of his grip. His other hand presses to her cheek the jagged jaw of a smashed bottle. He wields the bottle in the air, hoovering a shower of shards from every corner of the kitchen, then whips it up from the counter edge.

Her face twists into his fist, as he clamps her chin.

He throws her from him, moves away.

Three steps, two steps, one.

By now, he's a stranger – though this has happened before. It's like someone flicking a switch. It happens so quick, the curse on his lips is stillborn as a snarl and hiss: 'F –.'

The bin hurls up a bottle, which spins bottom-top-bottom-top to her hand till she has it by the neck. Her eyes lock with his, she pulls her foot up from the pedal of the bin.

He says she's asking for it – and maybe this time, she is.

There's this question mark fizzling away inside her like the fuse on a stick of dynamite. She needs to know more than a blue plus or minus sign on a white plastic wand can tell her. She needs to know who she's dealing with, how far he'll go, then she can do whatever she has to. She's never before felt this crazed – or so ruthlessly sane.

There's no making sense of it, except that it has *something* to do with her being late – with the pregnancy test in her bag – *something* to do with survival being non-negotiable, and life being precious.

But she has no real idea what she's doing when she backs up to the sink and holds his bottle horizontal. She knows only that she must stare him straight in the eye, stand firm, grip that bottle like it's the last thing she'll do, and let it gulp up every last drop of liquid, till it's full.

Young Girl with a Flower Basket

Sold at auction in 2018 for $115 million.

I would have refused in no uncertain terms if Mother hadn't come back from the *préfecture de police* wearing Agent Cousin's boot print on her backside. But she did. And two weeks later, there she still was: as good as branded, in purple, black and blue.

She'd been not-quite-there since she got back, and there was no talk to be had from her, so I wasn't sure what she was after when she reached into the filthy nest of ribbons she calls her glad rags, pulled out a dirty pink scrap and called me over. I went readily enough – it was the first thing she'd asked since her release – but I was quickly wary. Instead of saying, 'You keep your thieving little hands out, d'you hear?' she began tying the ribbon round my hair.

'You're hurting me,' I said. 'You've got hands like a vice-squad pig.' I yanked my head back, shook out my hair and stood, waiting to hear, 'You belong in a workhouse.' Or, 'You'll be doing time at Saint Lazare as soon as you're old enough.' But no words came. I turned sharply. Mother didn't flinch, didn't blink. She stared, her eyes red-rimmed but dry, as if she couldn't muster tears.

'Get your Sunday best,' she said, meaning my shawl.

'Sunday best, is it? Are we going to Mass then – on a Friday night?'

I waited – hoped – for her to say, 'Saucy-tongued little vixen', but again the words didn't come. Mother looked at me like she looks at the empty tea caddy, willing dust to form leaves.

When we set out, the shacks were creaking with cold and the donkey steps jutting from the dirt were slickening with frost. We slipped as much as we stepped out of the Maquis. Mother limped, moving like a badly worked puppet, but her face showed no pain. It showed nothing at all, for that matter. I didn't bother asking where we were headed, though I did wonder, with Mother staring ahead so intently, not bothering to part the brambles before moving through them.

With each step, cold knifed my toes where my boots had split. It got me thinking about Mesdames Rinette and Aude, who I met when they were out 'taking the air', and how Madame Aude was suspiciously kind, talking of getting newspaper to stuff my boots, what with winter setting in, and then too quiet whenever I passed. So I called out, 'Please gentleman, please kind lady, do buy my flowers...' louder and louder, moving in closer, till I could hear Madame Aude saying: 'Her mother was registered when she was taken in. Now she'll need the medical, else she won't get her card stamped.'

'It'll cost her three francs for the pleasure of having them peer up her skirts,' said Madame Rinette.

They might have been talking of any number of women in Montmartre, but for some reason I thought of the money Mother and I didn't have for bread and tea – or flowers to sell.

'She got bruising and a limp for free, and her spirits all but knocked out of her,' said Madame Rinette. I moved in closer still, though the thought that they might be talking about

Mother made me want to run and retch. Aude hushed Rinette, turned to me and said, 'Pretty as your posies, you are.'

'*Please* buy my flowers,' I said to Aude, knowing she couldn't, since sores round her mouth slowed her trade – for I won't be pitied by her or anyone.

When Mother and I reached rue Saint Vincent, I realised we were headed for Madame Petitdemange's – although I think I already knew. My 'Sunday best' weighed heavy on my shoulders and the pink ribbon seemed to tighten round my head. Though the cobbles were treacherous, and despite being club-footed with cold, I'd have gladly fled. I looked up and down rue des Saules, and back and forth along rue Saint Vincent, but I could go nowhere – not with Mother the way she was, staring straight ahead without looking at anything.

Her silence made me blather. 'The holly will be fruiting. I could sell holly. The berries are pretty as rowan – not so nice as snowberries, but still... There might be wild flowers to be had in the Maquis. Nothing's as hardy as scrubland flowers, even in winter. I could go first thing. I'll find something. *Something* to sell...'

Mother limped across the cobbles with unblinking determination. My breath started to come too quick and my mind scurried like a trapped rat trying to find some way out. I took one dead end and another, then my mind conjured up the image of Monsieur Max Jacob, of all things. A sunny day, rue Ravignan. The plane trees leafy and full. And Monsieur Jacob dressed so fine, with his waistcoat and monocle, as if he'd escaped his own days for a more elegant time past. He treats me fine too. Talks so fine...

Just the other day, it was the language of flowers. He said each bouquet in my basket was a poem. He looked at me, his kind, dark eyes searching mine, as if to check I believed. For a moment, though Monsieur Jacob is old enough to be my father – and for all I know he or any man in Montmartre might just be – I felt much, much older than him.

He tried to give me a bookful of words: '*Manual for Children of Mary*,' he said. The cover was chestnut brown and the letters golden.

'It's… beautiful,' I said.

'As are you,' said Monsieur Jacob, and my cheeks prickled. He said it so gentle. Not like most of them with their 'Got anything sweeter than roses, pretty?' I wanted to be a gentlewoman for him. His kind of lady. So I didn't say I can't read. 'I'm better with numbers than words,' I said. He touched his fingers to his temples, as if he had a sudden headache. Then he looked at me very directly and said, 'You could be better, Mademoiselle Linda. Better at reading, writing *and* arithmetic. Better in other ways. In *all* ways. You could enrol in the Children of Mary Immaculate.'

Each 'better' and 'could' cranked the world open like an accordion. It felt like looking out at a clear night sky, when the moon is a mother-of-pearl brooch fixed almost low enough to be picked and pocketed, and the stars are so many they might be stolen by the sackful. But what do you say to a big open sky? I just stood, taking it in. I thought of Madame Petitdemange's canary, so used to its cage that when she opens the door, it sits stupid, not sure what to do.

And that's how I was when we reached Madame Petitdemange's and her front door opened. She came herself to welcome us, smiling with lips too red and too many teeth. The colour bled into cracks round her mouth. There was that close-air smell – skin and breath, and whatever it is that's sweeter than flowers that the women put on their skin. Sickly. I stood on the threshold, unable to run, unable to enter.

Mother didn't push me, but it felt like that. Or perhaps it

was Madame Petitdemange pulling. Either way, I was taken in.

Madame held me by the wrist, pulling me quickly past the room on the right – but not so fast that I didn't catch sight of a man with a smart suit and cane, seated with a frilled-up woman on his knee and his hand down her front, digging about like he might pull up turnips. I looked away. Not because I hadn't seen it before. More because the colours alone are enough to make you queasy. The glinting green snake-eye glow of a glass of absinthe, lips and cheeks rouged like poppies, yellow fire blazing too bright in the sooty murk... I made for the kitchen where I usually wait with the maid, but Madame didn't let me go. It was Mother who slipped away down the corridor, while Madame led me on by the elbow, upstairs.

As we climbed, everything got closer: walls, stairs, air. After three short flights my own chest felt tight. We reached an attic room where a man sat back, kingly, on the single chair, his belly falling like a half-moon between his breeches. Beside him: an iron bed. Beneath that: a chipped chamber pot, decorated with red-hearted mignonette. The man looked at me and exchanged a nod with Madame, who then whipped me out so fast, I thought I was in trouble. She held my arm hard enough to hurt, but her eyes were kind and serious. 'There'll be blood after, but not so much you need worry,' she whispered.

I had no time to ask what she meant before she pushed me back in, and closed the door.

Even scampering between front door and kitchen, you hear noises at Madame Petitdemange's: groans, animal yelps. Through a door crack I once saw a woman's head lolling, her eyes half closed like she was dead.

So I knew it would hurt.

First, the man hurt me with his hands. His finger had this hard bit of skin or nail that snagged like a thorn. The rest hurt

51

worse. I fixed the image of the chamber pot in my mind, tracing and retracing the mignonette flowers, as if sorting them for a bouquet. I imagined mixing them with primroses, peonies, and pinks. I imagined lily of the valley, violets, and lavender. Roses. Moss roses. China roses. Roses, roses. Roses sell well. Something sweet. People love something sweet…

By the end I had such a basketful of bright red blooms that when I saw blood, I thought my mind had leaked. I remembered what Madame had said, but even then, the sight was shocking. My blood a bright red flower blooming on the bed. My blood so red it blanched the yellowing sheets.

I tugged my skirts across, to cover the stain. Needlessly, perhaps; when I looked to the man, his back was already turned.

*

'Out? Which one this time?' said Mother, with enough sniff and snarl to sound almost her old self.

'The Spaniard,' I ventured, but she was already gone wherever she goes when she gazes into empty space. I searched her face for Mother as I remember her, decking herself in chipped paste-diamonds to make her eyes sparkle, smoothing her hair into coils so whatever mean light we had bounced around her face. I found only her new self, all shadow and droop. Her mouse-nest hair. The crusty folds of the clothes she never takes off any more, not even at night.

'Be sure to move, even if it pains you,' I said, peering into her eyes. I wondered if she remembered how it used to be: her going out and me left behind. How, one time, I didn't want her to go, and I said that with her hair the way she'd done it, she looked like a dog. She'd grabbed me, but instead of slapping, pressed me to her, saying, 'I wish I could stay.'

But Mother showed no sign of remembering anything. She sat still, stared through me.

'Sit and rot then, and may the devil take you,' I thought – and would have said, if I had any hope left of riling her. I touched Mother's hand and found it cold as well-water despite the heat. I put my shawl across her, tucked it in, and turned to go. But knowing that on my return I'd find her where I'd left her, I turned back, tucked the shawl in tighter and said, 'Be sure to move, else you'll seize up.'

Mother looked at me then – a look of such startled recognition that it unsettled more than it pleased. She teased a grubby pink ribbon from the scrap heap on the side, pulled me down towards her, and tied it round my hair. I didn't know what she meant by this – if she meant anything at all. But I determined to take it as a gift of sorts, and held myself still though my stomach tightened like a fist.

Outside, crushing heat. Not a whisper of air stirred the nettles; butterflies sat wings spread as if pinned. The sun hammered down so hard, the broken brim of my hat seemed to sag beneath the weight of it. And heat rose from the dirt too. I felt it through boots, stockings and bloomers, as if my skirt was a chimney stack. Syrupy sunlight slowed my every step on the way to the studios off rue Ravignan. The thought of a chance meeting with Monsieur Jacob slowed my step still more but the very same thought quickened my heart, so I spun like a top between hope and dread till I felt sick and faint.

If Monsieur Jacob were to see me, he would swing his cane in greeting and call, 'Mademoiselle Linda! Are you not at place du Tertre today? What of your flower basket?' And because word spreads like pox in Montmartre, and because he and the Spaniard can often be seen together in the street or tumbling out of the Lapin Agile in the small hours, I would have to say,

'I'm come to see Monsieur Pablo.'

Monsieur Jacob would know why. *Might he imagine worse?*

I would be far from his hopes then. Far from his kind of lady.

The sun seems to burn harder, like a punishment. I swing my arms to show how little I care, how I'll be whatever sort of lady I please. But as I move, my armpits hiss out the stinking truth of me.

At rue Ravignan, the concierge is stationed by the door leading to the studios.

'Pablo the Spaniard,' I say, before she can ask my business. She looks me up, down, and spares no words of welcome but moves aside to let me enter. I pick my way down the rickety stairs, thinking all the time of Monsieur Jacob, and trying hard not to, giddy with the desire to chance upon him and to avoid any such thing. Creaking timbers betray my every step along the labyrinth of corridors. It is some comfort to think, as I do when I pass these walls festering with mould, the planks of wood piled high and rotting, the corners that stink of tomcat, and the scaly communal fountain, that the artists and poets of Bateau-Lavoir live no better than we in the Maquis.

At the Spaniard's door, I knock quietly so as not to attract the attention of Monsieur Jacob should he be passing, hoping all the while that he might. Monsieur Pablo opens, appearing fully and suddenly in the doorway. Though this is the third time I've come, the sight of him astonishes: eyes and hair dark as Monsieur Jacob's top hat, shadows dug deep in his cheeks, and a strong line from nose to mouth like a lion.

He greets me with two quick nods and hurries me inside.

With the cracked panes, it's no cooler inside than out. I am almost glad at the thought of taking off my clothes but I know that when Monsieur Pablo lifts his chin to the rickety wooden chair to say it's time to undress, I'll be as angry as I ever am. In that moment, my hands always feel like someone else's.

So I take my time. It's not the Spaniard's till he's paid and since he'll pay only when he's finished, I slip behind his easel to see how far he's come along.

My sullen-faced twin stares back at me. There I am, etched out in grey lines and a first few splodges of dirty pink, beige and blue. Monkey-footed, donkey-legged, flat-chested me. There is nothing about the painting that pleases, except a few faint lines tracing out the ghost of a flower basket to come. I look to Monsieur Pablo with half a mind to say what I think, but he is preparing brushes and paints with his back turned.

Then he spins on his heels, lifts his chin towards the chair.

Now that I would like him to turn away, he doesn't. He watches as a cat might watch a mouse hole. Black eyes prodding and probing, as if to winkle out my every secret. Even the soles of my feet feel bare, exposed to each wood fibre and join.

And it's as I stand there stripped that I hear Monsieur Jacob's voice clearly through the thin plaster wall: 'Pablo, my friend? Are you in?'

My heart bounces against my ribs, stupid and joyous, as if it's me he's come for. Every other part of me knows to run, hide. I turn to my clothes – an impossible pile of blouse, bloomers, skirts and stockings on a chair that is one hundred, two hundred, three hundred kilometres from where I stand. I reach for them before I've left the spot, but they seem to fly still further at the thought that Monsieur Jacob might enter. See me. Like this. Naked as the day I was born. Flat-chested, donkey-legged, monkey-footed me. Not Monsieur Jacob's sort of lady. Not her at all.

But when I blink, it's the Spaniard's face that is close to mine.

His eyes are full of fire and he holds a paintbrush to his lips to say 'quiet'.

'Work,' he says. A hot, wet whisper like a slap on the side of my face. I think he's demanding that he work, not me, but that amounts to the same thing. He smacks the air to indicate that I must take my pose.

'Pablo?' says Monsieur Jacob, knocking louder. My heart strains. It would open the door if it could.

The Spaniard shakes his head so vigorously a lick of hair falls over his brow. He looks out from beneath it, black and thunderous with that lion-line from nose to mouth. I am more than ever a mouse in a hole. Trapped.

More voices – softer, getting fainter. Footsteps, walking away. With them goes the Linda that Monsieur Jacob sees. The 'me' that could be. She slips like a phantom through the walls. I try to track her with my gaze but see only walls pussed with damp and seeping despite the heat, a water bucket by a basin, a cot in the corner with a chamber pot beneath. And then Monsieur Pablo, huffing his hair from his eyes, tugging me back into pose by the chin as if I were a donkey in harness.

I stand till my ankles itch like nettle rash. Till a burn rises up my legs. Till my joints lock.

Still the Spaniard stares. I try to stare back. To tell him with my eyes that I too can judge. He is not so very much older than me. And his face is not handsome – too broad, with cheekbones too high to be from around here. But he's hidden by his easel, scratching and dabbing, and when he pops out, his black eyes burn as if he would leave of me only cinders.

This thought sparks something in my belly, which flares to the back of my throat. Something that refuses to be picked up and presented this way or that, something that will *not* be reduced to cinders. Dressing myself in the language of the 'could-be' girl of Monsieur Jacob I say, 'Rest.'

The Spaniard steps – stamps out from behind his canvas.

'Look!' he says, waving his paintbrush to and fro marking an imaginary line between his eyes and mine. He means I must look at him, because he wishes to look at me. That's what his money buys.

But he hasn't paid yet.

And even when he has, he won't have bought me.

I place on the floor the chipped pot he has me hold, and step out of pose.

'Rest,' I say. It comes out as much a command as a demand. Grand. Imposing. So fine, I feel all wrapped up in the sound of my own voice. Monsieur Pablo stares, as surprised as I am. I stare back. I am a mouse holding a lion in an eye-lock. Perhaps I too am a lion? The walls, water bucket, basin and cot watch on. Even the humming heat stills. I speak again. Not to Monsieur Pablo. More to Monsieur Jacob. Or myself. I speak the 'me' that I would be if I could.

'It's not often I do this.'

I take the Spaniard's place behind the canvas, intending to tell him he hasn't caught my likeness. But my own face stares back like a challenge. Eyes black with fury, but fear too – sizing me up. A stubborn jaw. A mouth that looks like it would spit vitriol, if the lips could open of their own accord.

I hold my gaze. Narrow my eyes. Clear my throat.

'Mother and I live almost on flowers when they are to be got.'

And I bite my tongue – too late. My mouth has betrayed me with 'almost' and 'when'...

Worse, Monsieur Pablo has painted the flowers – such a shocking red, the canvas shouts, 'Liar!' Each bright bloom proclaims that everyone knows about the man at Madame Petitdemange's – and others besides. Each blossom hollers the blood I tried to hide.

And yet they are lovely, those flowers. I would gather them in my arms, if I could, hold their sweet, fresh petals close. So many bright blossoms… A basketful. Enough to keep mother and me in bread and tea, if only they were real enough to sell.

In Conversation with Ana Mendieta

Does it feel right, if I address you directly, like this? I wouldn't presume, if you hadn't done likewise, through your work. I tried other voices, but this one felt the most natural: the gap between 'you' and 'I' seemed to create a space for you to slip into and emerge from.

I read somewhere that you were scared of heights. I'm acrophobic too; the slightest vertical perspective leaves me with skin yanked tight, pelvic floor draw-strung, and palms and brow flash-frosted with perspiration. Here's something strange I heard about acrophobia: while most phobias relate to fear of the perceived danger coming close, sufferers of acrophobia fear they might be drawn to approach the danger against their conscious will – *l'appel du vide*.

Is there any connection, I wonder, with the pull of those primal voids so important in your work: the womb and the tomb?

Thinking of gaps: an analysis of fraud-related speech showed that it is easier to lie by omission than by commission. 'Not saying' is easier than 'saying', apparently, so liars hedge around the truth with fuzzy statements and distancing language. Fraudulent statements also tend to be wordy, with more positive and fewer negative emotional words, as if the liar was trying to present the situation in a favourable light.

Poets are supposedly liars who speak the truth. I see your work more like that – in poetry, it is often in gaps that the truth breaks through. Short-story writers use a similar technique, leaving strategic gaps – *lacunae* – that readers invest with meaning, to complete the work. They also employ open endings that unfold in heart and mind after the story's end.

My favourite of your works is the one where you lie entombed at Yagul, naked but for a shroud of flowers. The scene speaks of death, of course, but vibrates with life. Sunlight falls from above, picking out the idiosyncrasies of the stones so that they become eloquent, with their juts, dents, and patches of lichen. Vegetation pushes up in the shadows, where the dusty earth is moist. White flowers sprout like rogue weeds beneath your arms and between your legs, frothing blossoms over your sex, breasts and face so that you both appear from and disappear into the scene. Though you lie corpse-like, you are alive, animated by a slight asymmetry that sets one foot off-kilter, and the tilt of a wrist that allows your hand to espouse your hip. Sunlight glosses your shoulder and shin. Whenever I see a reproduction of that work, I think of the lines of Dylan Thomas about lettering on gravestones hammering through daisies, and the life-giving sun breaking in, breaking down.

I know of this work only through reproductions. In that series, which you called *Siluetas*, your silhouette was gouged out of mudbanks, printed into snow, rummelled from sea sand, and then reclaimed by the earth. The photographs are mere records.

There are later works where you shaped earth into female forms stylised to the point of symbolism, the curves simplified to labial abstractions. As an art history undergraduate, many years ago, I was looking at images of these when a classmate peered over my shoulder. 'Vulval,' he said, with enough of a wink and sneer for me to wonder if he wanted to reduce your work to that – to make a hole in which to bury it. I said nothing, but returned to the image. Even as I looked, it birthed new forms: pudenda became buttocks, buttocks became breasts, breasts became a beating heart.

Here's something I heard about hearts: the form may be an ancient abstracted representation of female genitalia, which might explain why love hearts feature so highly in the doodles of little girls; they are repeating a coded incantation to a power that is theirs, but which goes beyond them, and from which they are estranged.

You called your earth-body works a dialogue between the landscape and the female body. You believed these works were the direct result of your having been torn from your homeland. At twelve you were exiled from your native Cuba, separated from your parents. You left a city marked by *métissages* of every sort, where even plasterwork came in a cacophony of colours – mint and hibiscus, banana and lime – to come to a place of prim white fences and Protestant churches. The locals of that small Iowa town must have seemed alien, with their beige hair and pinky-white skin. Even downtown must have seemed desolate, with its wide empty streets and those old-time, low-rise brick blocks, which, to you, would have looked new. No wonder you felt cast from the womb. Your art was a way to re-establish the bonds that united you to the universe, an obsessive act of reasserting your ties with the earth. You called this a reactivation of primeval beliefs in an omnipresent female force; a return to a maternal source that has the power to restore and heal the soul.

It was, you said, a manifestation of your thirst for being.

61

Here's another thing we have in common, you and I: we were raised Roman Catholic. For Catholics, the price of eternal life is a blood sacrifice re-enacted by the priest during the Mass. Here's a related theory that I found in an analysis of church architecture: the Mass is a manifestation of an institutionalised womb-envy, whereby the priest (who can only be a man) gives life to his congregation by means of a miracle performed in the seclusion of the apse. Once fortified and restored by the sacred body and blood, the congregation leaves the altar by the narrow passage afforded by the central aisle, which functions like a birth canal. The theory caught my imagination. At that time, I was being taught a lot about Freud, female artists and phallus-envy, but nothing about the pulsions that female generative power might inspire.

That classmate I told you about, the one who was sniffy about your work, he used to like Lucio Fontana, an artist who took a knife to his canvases, slashing into them gaping slits.

You were no stranger to violence: one of your earliest works was conceived as a response to the rape and murder of a fellow student. I made myself look up an image of this artwork, in which you appeared, to an invited audience, bound, stripped and smeared with blood. I wanted to look away, but could not – which I think was your point. You wanted to render present the invisible, ignorable victim, to create a space in which to address sexual violence against women.

In another early work you sluiced a sidewalk with blood to record the reactions of passers-by. As it turns out, they did just pass by. You were shocked. You had expected some sort of response, perhaps a call to the police. You were the sort of person who wanted to do something.

Here is a fact that I would like to say is irrelevant, but which

I fear is not: you were pretty. You had ferociously thick black hair, bright brown eyes, a vivacious smile, and a neat, curvaceous little figure. It must have flattered your husband's ego to have you by his side. You could have got by on looks alone, I think. A girl still can. But you would not be reduced to that. In a series of self-portraits, you mortified and distorted your face and naked body, crushing yourself against panes of glass and photographing the result: a nose pancaked, cheeks rollered, eyelids crimped, and breasts levelled to the same plane as the belly. By participating as the object of your work, you became its ungraspable subject, estranged surely even from yourself.

Your work was never just about you though.

I'm thinking now of that work where you play dress-up, inviting viewers to consider racial and gender bias. My favourite of the series is the one where you take shaved-off beard tufts and fix them to your face, appropriating the beard to challenge what this facial hair means. I just watched a video of your husband, where he wears a curious frill of a beard that leaves his chin exposed. Rather than thinking that your beard was like his, I found myself thinking that his was like yours – a testament to the power of that work.

This said, it will not surprise you that I knew of your husband's art before yours.

He was an absolute authority in his field when you met, recognised as a founder of the Minimalist school. You were talented and driven, but known only among initiates – 'emerging', as they say. You met at a gallery where he served on a panel titled 'How has [sic] women's art practices affected male artist social attitudes?'

I returned to his work as background research for this piece. (What would he make of that, I wonder: being your background?) As an undergraduate, I liked the idea of Minimalism;

all those straight lines and industrial-looking blocks intended to do nothing more than simply assert their presence. After the posturing and clamour of Abstract Expressionism, which I had studied just before, it was a relief and novelty to come across objects that had nothing to say. 'What you see is what you see,' as Frank Stella said. The works are not as neutral as they might seem, though; laid out in a path or plane, they tend to coerce spectators, controlling their usage and perception of space. Still, looking now, I find them mute, sterile.

I wanted to challenge my personal bias, so went looking for videos of your husband, to see what the artist had to say for himself.

In one video, he says he works on location – 'very much in the movie sense'. He claims the world as his studio. Speaking of his infamous pile-of-bricks sculpture, which caused such outrage in the tabloids, he laughs: 'Bad publicity is as good as good publicity.' He talks about exposure in another video too, saying that you have to be in the right place at the right time. He lists the many famous artists he knew personally. All but one are men. The woman artist is the only one that he describes as 'beautiful'.

Your husband's work had already passed into the canons of art history when you won the Prix de Rome: his work was 'done'. You may even have told him, 'Minimalism is over.' I cannot know if that is true, but I believe that you knew how to press people's buttons: I still cannot stomach some of your bloodier works.

It sounds like Rome suited you. You got your own studio and were working hard, expanding your practice by making objects such as human-sized trunk segments seared with silhouettes. You talked of cutting back on the drink and smokes, so nothing would get in the way of your work.

*

You and your husband had been drinking, on the night you died.

I know this, and many other things, about that night – but it is all so much padding, with a hole where the central truth should be.

I know your exact address in Greenwich Village: you lived on the thirty-fourth floor, 300 Mercer Street, in an artsy neighbourhood of cobbles and graffiti tags, trees lean as lamp posts, and fire escapes laddering z's down brick façades in mottled white, rust and oxblood. I know about your husband's supposed affairs, that you were maybe going to divorce him, and that your neighbours heard you both arguing violently.

I know that you left him with scratches on his face and arms.

A nearby doorman heard a woman cry 'No! No! No!' just before your body fell. You landed thirty-three storeys down, on the roof of a deli, with such impact that you left an imprint.

'*No! No! No!*'

Your husband was acquitted; his guilt was not proven beyond reasonable doubt.

A recording of his 911 call had him saying: 'My wife is an artist, and I'm an artist, and we had a quarrel about the fact that I was more, eh, exposed to the public than she was. And she went to the bedroom, and I went after her, and she went out the window.'

She went out the window. Now there's a gap.

His story later changed. He told police that you and he had been watching television, then you went to bed, alone. When he went to bed, he found that you were gone, and the bedroom window was open. Your death was a tragic accident or suicide. Your husband's lawyer said that any seeming inconsistency in your husband's account of what happened was a result of his 'eclipsing' events the night of your death.

An eclipse is also the obscuring of one celestial body by another.

You were a rising star at the time of your death. 'Lesser known' than your husband, said reports of the murder trial, but 'gaining prominence'. It is frustrating that you might still be described this way, ever 'emerging'.

But you have not been eclipsed.

Your husband has retired, having 'made his statement'. You, however, are still 'working', busier than ever.

Your prices are up. Though many of your artworks remain, by their nature, unpossessable, photographs of them fetch five-figure sums.

You exhibit too. One recent exhibition blurb said that you had become a symbol. I made a note to myself not to make the same mistake. Keep the focus on her work, I noted. But then I turned again to your work and was met with a symbol: a female form fashioned from mud. She lies totemic, with one arm raised in what could be warning, salutation or blessing. The work speaks viscerally, like a beat pulsed through the earth. I find solace and strength here – an inexhaustible source, since it seems to keep coming, and coming.

I looked up the word symbol, and found that it comes from Latin and Greek. The etymology ties it to 'token' or 'mark'.

I am looking again at one of your *Siluetas*. As ever, the reproduction in my hands is only a token; the earth took to itself the original. The reproduction offers a view of the work, and marks my distance from it. Though I hold your work in my hand, it escapes me. And though you left this mark, and are present by it, when I look into the picture, I cannot find you there. Just as the earth subsumed your work, so the work subsumes you.

Yet from this gap that you created, this void, you keep springing forth, ungraspable.

Feeding is Forbidden

It's a pigeon. *Just* a pigeon. Deep breath, deep breath, deep breath. Those legs! My God! One foot all gnarled, like a leper – no bell, mind. Just right there, in your face. Skin so pink it looks naked. Utterly obscene, but there it is marching up and down the windowsill like it has business there. Feathers the colours of Paris. Sodden skies, zinc roofs, dirty pavements. Splodges the colour of stuff you'd swerve to avoid. Cocking its head now. Is it watching my hand? Wanting to get in on Cléa's carrot purée? Can it hear me thinking? It raises its tail as if in salute. And shits. Right there on the sill.

I give it the non-look I'd give a pushy rush-hour beggar on the line six commute, and turn back to Cléa's open mouth – to my impatient, lip-smacking Cléa. But the bird's still looking. Observing.

'Clé-ah!' I say, partly to show the bird I'm ignoring it. But I can't, quite. I put down the spoon and get up, leaving Cléa grasping at the air with her chubby starfish hands. 'Shoo!' I say to the pigeon, flicking a tea towel. It flaps off unhurriedly, drops down on to the roof opposite.

At first, it was the odd one or two, now it's – *how many is a flock?* A mob, more like, since someone on the fifth floor took to feeding them. They gather three times a day. You learn things like this, on maternity leave. You learn the secret rhythm of the city's stay-at-homes – and pigeons.

There they go. Up like jump jets. Then down on to that fifth-floor windowsill in a flurry of feathers. A flapping, forty-winged, twenty-beaked monster. The window opens, and a single gloved hand steals out. Bony fingers bunched into claws, protruding from a puff of fingerless glove. Skin so old and grey, it's sexless. But it's *got* to be the Chinese lady in the left-side apartment – it can't be anyone else. She lives alone. Her letterbox is labelled with the almost absurdly generic 'Dupont'. Her husband must've been French, I guess. The mystery is those gloves. She never wears them outside. Whenever she heads out, she's hatted and heeled. Skirts hemmed just so, to sit right on the knee. Chic, in a fusty, musty way. Always a '*Bonjour Madame*', a nod, a smile…

A cry. An open mouth. Cléa's pink tongue twitching in anticipation of the next spoonful.

'Clé-ah,' I say, depositing another load of orange gloop. I think about the Chinese lady, wonder whether pigeon-feeding feels for her like Cléa-feeding feels for me. And if so, is it like serving mashed banana, when little Cléa's eyes roll with pleasure, and you feel your heart – actually *feel* your heart – pumped so full of joy you hardly dare exhale in case it comes out suddenly and inappropriately like air from an unknotted balloon, and yet for all the swelling it feels lighter too, as if joy were some sort of emotional helium? Or is it more like now, when Cléa's got hand and spoon under close surveillance – and that intense feeding-time stare – as if we were both caught in some survival game that's oddly and uncomfortably impersonal?

'Clé-ah!' I say, turning my back on that unseemly thought. 'Is it nice?' More orange gloop. Nearly finished now. Scrape, scrape. Scoop, scoop.

'Shall we tell Papa about the pigeon?' I say. Cléa makes a fish-mouth and blub-blub-blubs. I will tell Alexandre, when he gets back. I'll work it into something of a story. I'll mention my purée – someone should – and how I felt something watching as I fed Cléa. I'll tell how I heard scratching on the sill, how my mind cooked up a nightmare that was outside, trying to get in. 'It was *right* there at the window!' I'll say.

'Eh?' I say to Cléa, heaving her onesied babybod on to my hip for our little look out before naptime. From the window, I see the Chinese lady, there in the courtyard. Loitering, I'd say, if she weren't so dainty. Or waiting? For what or who?

She looks up, sees us. Finger-flutters a wave.

'Shall we say hello, Cléa? A hello before bed-byes?' I take Cléa's fat little arm and flap it for her.

*

'It was a shock, right there at the window!' My voice comes out taut and foreign-sounding – too full of emotion. And this may be because all I got for my heart-warming tale of homemade organic carrot purée was a peck on the forehead, and when I said 'Alexandre!' he looked at me blankly, with the same expectant face as Cléa when she wants to be lifted from her cot. And it may also be because I was shifting Cléa on to my other hip at that particular moment, and she does this thing where she grabs a handful of me and won't let go till she's secure in her new position, and then only lets go to grab another piece of me – collar, hair, skin, whatever, which makes me feel a lot like I'm caught in some hideous host-parasite coevolution scenario. But you can't say that, can you? It doesn't do to shine too bright a light on things – to ruin the gentle glow of motherhood. So you end up saying things like 'It was a shock, right there at the window!' and sounding like a woman who's seen Freddy Krueger.

Alex bundles us, mother and child, away from the window, imposing his bulk between us and the rest of the world. It's new, this Tarzan impression – new since Cléa. I'm about to tease him with 'Me Jane' but when I open my mouth, I find that my chin's tucked in demurely, Jane-style.

Alex looks out, takes in the pigeons. His eyes narrow. It's a thirty-strong squad now, spread out with a regulation space between each bird, as if even they are embarrassed by their number and proximity. The mizzle's thickening into rain, and the pigeons are already hunchbacked, hiding their heads. They look oddly human, bundled up like the sleeping-bagged figures you see hunkered down in doorways.

'Poor things,' I say. 'Out in all weathers.'

'There never used to be so many,' Alex says. His tone's so cold it sets off a flutter of protective panic in my heart, though for what or who, I couldn't say.

'It's getting out of hand,' he says. 'Someone must be feeding them.'

'But what if it's some poor old dear for who pigeon-feeding is –'

The fifth-floor window opens, a gloved hand creeps out. The pigeons rise like an Old Testament plague.

'*C'est illégal,*' says Alex. '*C'est* complètement *illégal.*'

*

Four o'clock, and I'm powering the pushchair across the courtyard cobbles, wondering if it will help get me my abs back, and looking down to check Cléa's cheeks, and thinking can

cheek-wobble cause discomfort in infants, and how this isn't a
question that ever arose at work, and are my pens still where I
left them on my desk, and what are my colleagues up to now,
and what's the goss round the coffee machine, and then it's
break. Stop. Because there's that lady from the fifth floor.

She raises two hands as if pleasantly surprised, but says,
'Is it that time already!' And turning to Cléa, says, '*Alors! C'est
l'heure de la promenade?*' She has no accent but handles words
carefully, as if French were a white guest towel that she was
scared of spoiling. Tipping her head to one side she makes a
closed-mouth smile so wide, her eyes all but disappear. She
hops about like a hen sparrow, more hopeful than expectant,
and I shoo from my mind the notion that my comings and go-
ings have been observed. She must be so lonely, to feed the
pigeons like she does. '*Bonjour Madame*,' I say, and smile.

'*Quel beau bébé!*' she says, as we pass. I keep hearing her saying it even when I'm halfway up the street. Even when I'm bundled on a bench, a proper distance from all the other carefully
spaced mums, nannies, grannies and au pairs – and well away
from the huddle of pro mums and carers that's always there,
yakking and flapping as they tear to pieces whatever miserable
scraps of gossip they've got. I *keep* hearing her say it. There was
something like desire in her voice. No, something more intense
and non-negotiable. Something like hunger, perhaps.

Poor thing.

*

Four o'clock. Pushchair, cobbles, abs, cheek-wobble…

And there she is – the lady from the fifth floor. Again. She
doesn't pretend to be surprised this time, but opens her arms in
gracious welcome.

'*Bonjour Madame! Comment allez-vous?*' she says, and even as I'm saying, '*Bonjour Madame. Bien, merci. Et vous-même?*' she's touching me lightly on the arm. Such dainty bones they have, old ladies. They must be made of honeycomb, to weigh so little. She raises her hand, fingers fanned, to signal 'wait'. Smiling sweetly, she unclasps her bag – an old-time thing, all cracked varnish and creaky mechanics. Clasp and hinges begrudgingly oblige, the bag squawks open, Madame dips in a hand, and from the depths produces a tiny origami stork. She flips my hand, which feels suddenly too big, and places the stork in my palm, saying, 'For you.' Producing an even smaller stork, she says, '– your little one. A gift.'

The sight couldn't be more marvellous if the birds had flown from the skies to alight in my hand. They're so precisely folded, such perfect creations. Almost as beautiful as Cléa's little ears and lashes – and I get that same rush of emotion, looking at them – a feeling that something inside has taken flight. So when she suggests tea, I accept.

*

The air smells of overripe roses and mildew. Madame Dupont fusses in a corner by a thinly covered, tidily made single bed. From beside the bed, she heaves out an ancient heater. She clicks its heavy switch; the heater sparks, and wheezes out carbonised dust.

'Sit, sit,' says Madame, showing me to one of her two chairs. Then she flitters to her kitchenette.

On the mantel is a clock labouring each tick and tock, and a clouded stem vase, in which a rose hangs its head. At each end sits a frame: one is dark, polished wood; the other silver, polished to gilt. Between the chairs stands a rosewood coffee table, with tapered legs and mottled brass-capped feet. The only other furniture, if you can call it that, is a Singer sewing machine. On its burnished surface sits a box, spilling ribbon and lace. Those fingerless gloves come to mind, triggering the queasy cocktail of knowledge-lust and self-revulsion that I usually only feel when stalking on social media or faced with mirrors lit too cruelly bright; I consciously avoid looking for them.

'What clever hands you must have, to make things,' I say, but Madame Dupont doesn't hear me above the quaking of the tea-tray that she's laying shakily on the table.

'Let me?' I say.

'You have your little one,' she says firmly.

Fearing that I might have offended, I say, 'What fragrant tea! Is it Chinese?' Madame Dupont looks blank for a second – long enough for embarrassment at my ethnic pigeonholing to paint my cheeks pink. But Madame Dupont nods, smiles, and deftly turns my conversational crumbs into cake, which she serves back to me: 'India,' she says. 'Indian tea. It's *very* good. And the porcelain, I brought with me from *Indochine*. Long ago. I have been here since. Nine. Teen. Forty. *Eight!*' She delivers each number like a surprise gift, her eyes twinkling. Leaning towards me – that light touch on the arm again – she whispers, 'I remember when there was one shared toilet for *all* the apartments on the floor.' She giggles, and her hand flutters to her mouth. Cléa, gurgling, reaches out to Madame Dupont, whose eyes light up. She pecks kisses into Cléa's palm – so greedily that I'm not sure if it's giving or taking, and I hold Cléa tight round her giggling, wriggling middle.

When the kissing is done, my eyes slip back to the picture frames. Madame Dupont brings them to me, and points to the wooden frame. A young man looks out unsmiling. His collar is crisp, his tie tight.

'My husband. He was a soldier. In *Indochine*. Now Vietnam, Cambodia, and Laos.'

'*Indochine*,' I say, letting the word whoosh me through time and space, far beyond my little window, my little Paris.

'You know it?' says Madame Dupont. I can only shake my head.

'My son,' says Madame Dupont, pointing to the once-silver frame. A boy looks directly at me. His hair is parted ruler-straight, like his father's. His eyes are liquorice-coloured like his mother's, but have none of her sparkle.

'My daughter,' she says. A docile-looking girl stands behind her brother, staring into the middle distance. Her smooth hair is held back with a bow. 'My girl's gone,' says Madame Dupont. I must look horrified, because she hurries to add, 'No, no, not *gone* – flown.' Her hands gesture a bird in flight. 'She lives in the south. My son is in Paris. A lawyer. Very busy. Very, very busy!'

By now Cléa is squirming, so I sip the last of my tea.

'Well, this has been lovely!' I say.

'More tea?' says Madame Dupont.

'Thank you, but we must be going. There's the shopping to be done, supper –'

'A biscuit? I have some, somewhere…'

'No, really, Madame Dupont.'

As I stand to go, Madame Dupont says, '*Attendez!*' She flits to her Singer, opens her sewing box, and takes from it a doll, which she holds out. The doll's features are so finely embroidered, I almost expect her to blink. Her wool hair is coiffed with a ribbon, tied in a perfect bow. Beneath her skirts are frothy lace-trimmed knickerbockers and petticoats.

'You made this?' I say. Madame Dupont smiles, nods.

'For your little one,' she says. 'I will make a hat too, so she can dress dolly to go out.'

74

'It's too beautiful, Madame Dupont. She's too young.'

'I will make a hat and give you the doll, with the hat, next time.'

'It's too much.'

'Next time,' she says. And then again. And as I thank her one last time for the tea, and step on to the landing, she's still chirping, 'Next time, next time…'

*

Four o'clock.

Quarter past.

Twenty.

Madame Dupont's *still* there. Pottering about as if the courtyard were some sort of ornamental garden, ready to descend on me like a hungry, hundred-strong flock as soon as I step outside. There she is, armed with a handbag full of origami storks and carefully embroidered dolls.

Despite Cléa digging her heels into my haunches, I stay back from the window, out of sight, until I'm sure Madame Dupont has gone.

When I do slip out, it's on tiptoes with Cléa strapped tight to me. We've almost made it to the other side of the courtyard, when I gasp. Break. Stop. There's a fluster of mangled wing, beak, and claw on the floor – so close that I back up to the wall. It's a pigeon. *Just* a pigeon. *Deep breath, deep breath, deep breath.* The bird stumbles on bloodied feet, one wing trailing. *Why do they* never *die? Why go limping about like an affront?* The bird flaps clumsily to a corner, huddles behind a drainpipe. I look into its orange eyes and it stares back, like something from a Wild West shoot-out – like it's it or me. I inch past, and it pushes against the plasterwork as if to flatten itself. My panic subsides.

I manage to think, 'Poor thing.' *But what can you do?*

I go on my way.

When we return, there's no sign of the bird – thank God. Still, I edge along the courtyard walls, holding Cléa close. It's only when we're safely behind our own closed door that I breathe out properly, relieved.

*

'Clé-ah!' I say, because she won't take gloop from Alex otherwise. She follows me with her eyes, as if my hands were her property.

'It was *right* there in the courtyard!' I say, picking up my story about the dying pigeon.

'It's got to stop,' says Alex. 'For that woman's sake, as much as anyone else's. She rents.' As president of the co-proprietors' association, Alex knows things like this.

'You can get thrown out for pigeon-feeding,' he says. 'Her landlord would love that. She must be the only person in Paris still protected by the 1948 rent caps, so she's paying a pittance. People would kill to pay so little to live in central Paris.'

Those fingerless gloves come to mind. *Is she all alone? Can she pay for heating?*

'I'll put up a notice,' says Alex.

'Don't.'

'If that doesn't work, I'll get her reported.'

'Don't, please,' I repeat and the ridges in Alex's brow melt.

'I'll talk to her,' I say.

*

'Clé-ah!'

She lip-smacks.

'Clé-ah!' I deposit another load – brown gloop today.

'Clé-ah!' I say again, because it's too quiet.

There's no sound but the scraping of the spoon. No scratching on the sill. And on the wall, there's the odd bird, but so few I wonder if there's been an outbreak of avian flu. *Is Madame Dupont's window stuck? Is she sick – or worse?* Into my mind flashes an image of Madame Dupont, face-down on her ancient lino, arms spreadeagled as if flying face-first into the floor.

'Shall we go see Madame Dupont, Cléa? Shall we?' But Thursday's baby massage. So tomorrow then. Tomorrow we'll go.

*

'What do you think, Cléa?' She blinks clueless at my cake. It seems to fall apart even as I look at it. It's not a cake. It's a loose association of crumbs that would rather have nothing to do with each other. But there's no time to make another. I batch it up, wrapping the aluminium as carefully as my big hands allow. With the 'cake' in hand, and Cléa perched on my right hip, we head off, downstairs, across the courtyard.

Standing with his back to me is a silver-haired man, too smartly suited to be here during the day. He belongs in some high-ceilinged office in the sixteenth *arrondissement* or behind glass walls in La Défense. He seems to be overseeing a man in overalls, who is carrying one box while shoving another into place to prop open the door to the street. He could be moving in, but looks more 'landlord' than 'leaser'. So why the boxes?

By the drainpipe, I see a Singer sewing machine. Into my mind dart the words 'denunciation' and 'eviction', followed by a flurry of accusations: 'You said you'd talk to her but you didn't, and now it's too late…'

I manage to dress up my panic as neighbourly enquiry: '*Excusez-moi, Monsieur, c'est Madame Dupont qui déménage?*'

The man turns, looks directly at me. Almond eyes, liquorice black. Though he's middle-aged, I recognise the boy in Madame Dupont's photo frame. He gives a headshake so conclusive, my heart sinks.

'Madame Dupont —?' I murmur, unable to formulate the question. I find myself raising a hand to cover Cléa's face.

'Yes. Sad. Very sad,' he says. His words are quick. Clipped. He could be announcing the quarterly financial results.

'I'm so sorry.'

'There's nothing anyone could have done.'

'*Je suis désolée,*' I say again, but he has turned to face the man in overalls.

At the park, I throw away the cake. Beneath an incongruously blue sky, I walk circuits, pointedly ignoring people and pigeons and anything else that looks too alive, bringing down my heels hard as if to punish the paths. I walk and walk, till Cléa air-pedals her feet against my hips, demanding to go home.

When we return, the sewing machine has gone. I stand by the drainpipe for a long time, stupidly looking for it, feeling desolate and unwhole, wanting to fill the empty space with whatever it was I'd been holding back — whatever it was that I was too scared or too mean to give.

*

'Clé-ah!' The gloop's from a pot — not even organic — and the cake things are still out. There are crumbs everywhere. Everywhere.

'Clé-ah!' I say, half hoping the sound will summon pigeons. But there's no scratching on the sill. No cooing on the wall.

Cléa clamps her mouth shut, and I don't have the heart to cajole it open; I don't feel like eating either.

I get up from the table and gather the corners of the crumby tablecloth.

'Shall we feed the pigeons, Cléa?' I say, opening the window. I release two corners of the cloth, which is claimed by the air. For a fleeting moment, it becomes a picnic blanket set in the sky. Then I give it a hearty, two-handed flick, and shake out all the crumbs.

Women's Business

Doctor Cartier is more expensive than I can afford. Instead of a bunch of flowers at reception, there's a floral composition. But the receptionist's frosty smile tells me that I've come to the right place. Her mouth and nails are bright blood red. Against her white blouse and skin, they look like neatly contained little murders.

'May I have the name under which you made the appointment, please?' she says.

I give my name, and wonder why her question left wiggle room – if many women make appointments under maiden names, without telling anyone else.

'Referral,' I add, though she hasn't asked – and it's not exactly true.

'Cartier is one of the best in Paris,' my general practitioner told me, almost apologetically. 'I can recommend other specialists who wouldn't cost so dear.'

'No,' I said. '*À la guerre comme à la guerre.*'

So my GP did not direct me here; I chose.

The receptionist drums on her keyboard, sees I'm here for a check-up.

'*Ah oui,*' she says. '*C'est pour le contrôle demandé par le docteur Dubois.*'

81

'*Oui, le contrôle,*' I say.

'*Le contrôle,*' she repeats, and I wonder if I've said more than I meant to – if she's understood not just what I'm here for, but also why.

The receptionist shows me to the waiting room, where everything is hard-edged. Ceiling and floor are incised with scalpel-slit straight lines that intersect at right angles. Metal frames keep the sag of the leather chairs in check. The corners of the side table could kill.

There's satisfaction to be had from this – a certain reassurance. But it's not enough; when I close my eyes, even just to blink, I still see the division of cells: soft-skinned alien eggs from inner space, slowly stretching, pulling apart, multiplying… It was the same when I got pregnant – only then, it felt like a private viewing of the Big Bang. Now, it's a vision of the enemy.

From an obsidian stack of art magazines I take the top slab, and flick through too fast. I learn that the damask rose was brought to Europe by crusaders, and that Spartan women who died in childbirth were buried with the honours of soldiers killed in battle. When I come to a full-page print of a Barbara Kruger masterpiece, I stop. In white lettering set against 999-emergency red, it hollers: 'Your body is a battleground.'

I look quickly left, right, all around as if the assailant might be hiding in the waiting room rather than lying low inside me. The receptionist raises an eyebrow.

'*Puis-je avoir de l'eau, s'il vous plaît?*' I say, asking for water so courteously it sounds like a cover-up, even to me.

The receptionist indicates the water fountain, and offers, '*Un petit café?*'

I nod, smile. She slips out, and returns with an impeccable white cup.

'*Je vous remercie,*' I say, still playing the polite guest. As I take the cup, I wonder why I am holding out my little finger. A crusader's bloodied hand comes to mind, pinching a rose stem delicately between forefinger and thumb. I look down at the coffee – at the tightly packed espresso froth – and see bubbles of life in deepest, darkest space, pulling apart till they pop into two, four, eight, multiplying in time to some cosmic beat, clustering, teeming... I knock back the coffee. One swallow, bitter as bile.

The pleasure lasts for longer than that though; the coffee is chased by a burn like a blast from a blowtorch, scalding from throat to belly. But even as I'm savouring this satisfaction, it is more than matched by bloodlust: I want the burn to go lower – down, right down... To shock and awe my body into submission.

Control, I think. *Self-control.* I slow-breathe, to pacify my mutinous heartbeat.

I felt this irrationally fierce once before. I was just pregnant, and had told no one. It wasn't planned. I was investigating options, so I could say it had been my choice. And this guy came too close on the metro – at least that's how it felt. I had to chew my bottom lip to stop myself snarling, and could easily have gone at him teeth bared, talons out. I was surprised by this sudden awareness of my nails and canines, but I realised then that I'd made my choice. Or that I didn't have as much choice as I wanted to lay claim to. What I knew in my belly was this: if I was drowning, I'd slash my stomach with whatever was to hand, be it butter knife or rough-edged stone; I'd claw open my womb with my nails if need be, and I'd rip out my child and hold her above the waves, that she might live.

'I want to keep the baby,' is how I explained that to my husband. I tried to smile sweetly, like the cradle-gazing mother in that Berthe Morisot painting. I had qualms of course – wondered if I should have invited him to share from the start in the messy business of deciding over life and death. I still don't know who I was protecting – our daughter, him, or me. But when his poor sweet mouth turned infantile with shock – horror and delight all at once – I was glad I'd offered him my best effort at a rosebud smile.

A phone rings. The receptionist engages in a murmured exchange, then leads me to the surgery door. Doctor Cartier greets me with a gaze that is blue and pitiless. Her handshake leaves me feeling delightfully frostbitten. With a chin-raise, she directs me to the chair by her desk.

'First, let me explain,' she says.

Although her tone makes it clear that the 'let' is purely decorative, I nod.

She tells me about cervical cellular anomalies and how they are graded. She sketches a diagram. I see the neat partitions of a garden *à la française*, where nature is subject to the ruler, divided, controlled. Or a military situation map. She points to lines from which anomalies are considered pre-cancerous or cancerous.

'Beyond this, they must be removed,' she says. 'By electro-surgical loop, laser, or cold-knife excision.'

Cold, I think. *Knife*.

'Do you understand?' she says.

Her blue eyes stare, unblinking.

I understand that she needs me to tick the terms and conditions box with another nod, which I cede.

'I like to explain everything,' she says. 'To give the patient ownership.'

And with that, she wrong-foots me. No longer myself, I am now a patient. Somewhere between home and here, I have lost my name.

Doctor Cartier stands.

'Undress,' she says. 'Lie down.'

I lie knees together, arms crossed. Then I remember this

pre-natal check-up where a doctor asked me, as I lay supine, if I wanted to know what breastfeeding was like. I figured I'd breastfeed so I nodded 'yes'. And she tweaked my nipple. Hard. Just like that. At the time, it felt like nipple rape. But my daughter came at me just the same way – like a snapping turtle, hungry for human flesh. So maybe it *is* better to know – to go in owning that much, at least?

I part my knees, press my feet harder into the stirrups.

'*Prête?*' says Doctor Cartier.

She doesn't wait for an answer before inserting her state-of-the-art equipment. Her monitor fills with the much-magnified pink and red shininess of my insides. My mind free-associates, confuses this with a pre-natal ultrasound, and for a split second, I seek the heartbeat of the beloved spaceman visiting my body. Then I remember what my body is gestating now.

'Last time I saw myself like this, I was pregnant,' I say. It's an attempt at gallows humour, but Doctor Cartier does not smile. She does not turn from her monitor.

'Pregnancy starts the same way,' she says. 'With the mutation of cells.'

I almost cobble together some joke about how consent should be a prerequisite to both states. Almost say that the pink-edged pregnancy leaflets never made the comparison. But Doctor Cartier is shaking her head like a cartographer faced with tricky terrain. She relabels the land in her own language:

'Severe dysplasia,' she says. '*Carcinoma in situ.*'

Still, it is only when she says, 'There *is* confusion as to where to draw the line between the two,' that I realise I have been dropped behind enemy lines – that labelling alone will not be enough to reclaim the territory. I say nothing, but press myself into the couch till a protective lip of padding rises around me.

'Dress,' she says, when she has finished.

I slip behind her screen and dress curled in on myself as if the screen were no bigger than a beach towel. With my underwear on, I skim a hand over arms, legs, earlobes – a sad inventory of things still uncolonised that maybe belong just to me. Then I pull on the too-thin protection of my summer dress and wrap my cardigan round me tight.

*

At reception I write a cheque that would normally make me wince, feeling only numb.

'I'll give you the scenic route to the metro,' says the receptionist, like I'm the sort of lady of leisure who can afford this place. 'There's a garden,' she says. 'You'll see. It's very pleasant.'

I follow her instructions unthinkingly, stupefied.

As I walk, I wonder how best to tell my husband about the operation to come. I imagine him moon-eyed, his jaw loosed as if the shock had come at him from the end a fist.

'It's the very earliest form,' I'll say. 'Just one grade off pre-cancer.' And I won't say 'cold-knife excision'. I won't even say 'operation'. I'll call it a 'surgical intervention'.

Then when I'm alone, I'll call my sister. She found a lump last year, so I will spare her nothing. I will reclaim the violence as mine. All the slash. All the burn. But I'll let her share in it.

'What happens if they don't eliminate the anomalies?' she'll want to know.

'They'll do another operation,' I'll say. 'Then another biopsy, to check. And then another operation, if they need to. They'll keep hacking away at me like so much salami, until the cells are obliterated.'

My kindly sister, sweet-natured mother of three, will pause. Then like a cold-blooded killer, she'll say one more word: 'Good.'

All Things Bright and Beautiful

'Have you ever seen a hamster before?' asked Anne Marie. Her voice was clean and clear, like when she was reading the bidding prayers, or answering in class. She reached a hand inside the cage and, with one finger, gently investigated a nest of straw. Emma lowered her head. She thought, 'No,' but held back the word, wanting to look at the question from all angles – to think what the consequences might be.

'Have you?' said Anne Marie.

Emma looked at her friend – at Anne Marie's face, beamy-bright and smiling, like the golden-haired children in the 'Suffer little children...' poster in church. The bottom of the poster said something about the kingdom of heaven belonging to such as these. With her white socks, neat plait, and short, white fingernails, Anne Marie was definitely such as these.

'*Have* you?'

Emma shook her head, keeping her face a blank.

'His name's Goldie,' said Anne Marie, as her fingers disappeared into sawdust and straw. They re-emerged, lightly curled around the hamster.

He was golden-brown and sagged like a beanbag, trimmed at each corner with a tiny pink foot – the smallest Emma had ever seen. His ears were tiny too, and folded and tucked so neatly they might have been made by fairy hands or God's tidiest angels. He had shiny, black-bead eyes. When Emma looked into them, he looked back and there was a sort of dancing spark inside: his own knowing and his own life. This so moved her that the sun seemed to come out all at once. Warm, melting, yellow light spread through her, almost all the way.

'They come from Syria,' said Anne Marie.

Emma thought that Anne Marie sounded young sometimes, though they were the same age. Anne Marie was always so sure of things: her turn to speak, what time she would be collected, whether something was allowed or not… That sort of sureness came from not knowing, like Adam and Eve before the apple. Emma knew too much, and not enough. Enough not to be sure of anything. Syria sounded unlikely: it was a place in the Bible, far away.

'You got him from Syria?'

Anne Marie shook her head – a quick, definite no.

Embarrassed, Emma dipped her chin so that she could peep out from behind her fringe.

'Hamsters. *Hamsters* come from Syria. But not Goldie,' said Anne Marie. 'We got him from Mear's Pet Supplies. They do fish – goldfish and stuff. Rabbits too, and mice, and sawdust, and pellets…' The list went on. *So no lie then*, thought Emma. Only the truth could come out like that, gushing like water from a tap.

She imagined Anne Marie in a confessional. Sins that made God only smile: a confession box full of not coming quick when Mummy called and forgetting to make her bed. She watched her friend's hands: one, cupped like a new flower, for the hamster to sit in; the other fluttering up like a butterfly, as Goldie clambered towards Anne Marie's wrist. Giggling, Anne Marie guided him to the cradle of her palm, where he reared on his back legs, revealing a plumped-pillow body, velvet paunch, and two tiny silk-gloved hands.

Emma let a smile lift her cheeks. Just looking at the hamster, she felt lighter and brighter, as if she could un-know, but she couldn't, quite.

'How do you know he's a boy?' she asked.

Anne Marie shrugged and sucked the end of her plait.

'They said so at the shop.'

He hasn't got a thingy, Emma thought.

'Do you want to hold him?' said Anne Marie, offering up Goldie as if he were a cupcake. Emma did, but she shrank into herself and shook her head. She feared that somehow, whatever was bright and beautiful in the hamster would know. Her hands would tell.

'Don't be scared,' said Anne Marie, coaxing her little cargo on to Emma's palm.

As Emma felt the barely there weight of him and the press of his minuscule paws, she filled with a rush of tenderness. It was like someone whispering to her a good secret. She felt so close to being one of the wise and wonderful that her chest welled and swelled with it.

'I'll get his exercise ball from the kitchen,' said Anne Marie. 'He might escape, so I'll close the door.'

Shadows lengthened in Emma's mind.

'I don't want −' she said.

But Anne Marie was already trotting to the door. 'I'll be right back,' she said.

With a click, the latch bolt slipped into its catch − a sound that made everything in the room jump closer. The fuzz above the carpet pile became as offensively intimate as someone's ear or nose hair, while the grain of wood on the table top stood out like distended pores. Emma held still, ears and eyes alert. Behind closed doors, bad things happened; she didn't know why, exactly, but sensed that there were reasons. She could feel guilt creeping up on her from behind, God breathing over her shoulder. She fancied she caught a whiff of His breath – that mix of shaving foam, shoe polish and incense that hung so heavy in the sacristy.

Emma peered down at the hamster, taking in the intricate lacework of veins in his ears, the thistledown hairs on his nubby pink tail. He washed his face, unaware.

She was alone with the danger. One-of-a-kind alone. Emma better understood Eve – why she'd wanted Adam to eat the apple too. Emma thought of Father Michael, when he squeezed his eyes shut as if in prayer, and she became sole witness to his eyebrows, dark and wiry, the bluish bulges beneath his lids, and that long nose, so shiny it seemed to strain towards its red and purple tip. Father Michael said God was all-knowing, all-seeing. But that only made it worse. If He turned a blind eye, it meant she deserved it.

Emma raised a finger, ran it down the semi-circle of Goldie's curved back. Perhaps to him, that was the hand of God?

Goldie lumbered towards her sleeve. She herded him down, trying hard to work her hands the way Anne Marie had. The very effort made her feel false, but Goldie settled in her palm, sure of the hand holding him. She felt the flutter of his heart, the shell-thin casing of his ribs, and realised what a terrible thing it is to hold a life. She became both great and small. Something inside bounced against her ribcage, like sunlight trying to nudge its way through cloud.

But even as the clouds broke, darker clouds rolled in. Emma knew what it was to feel small in a bad way. To be *too* small, constrained by someone stronger, held by force. Also, by her own body, frozen; knees that won't straighten on command, a rib cage that spasms rather than rises and falls.

She stroked her fingertip along the hamster's flank.

He started.

Whiskers stiff, nose snuffling, he probed the air where her finger had been. When Father Michael's eyes opened he always looked startled too, as if she had walked into the room without knocking. As if the hand clamping hers wasn't his at all.

Emma squeezed the hamster, just a little.

His feet scrabbled and his head strained. The thread of his spine flexed. It would thrash if it could, but she held it firm. She controlled two bodies now: hers and the hamster's.

The hamster's spine pulsed with effort, then relaxed.

Emma squeezed tighter, feeling the hamster's flesh filling out between her fingers. Still, the poor hamster didn't comprehend; its eyes bulged, dumb and desperate. She wondered how hard she'd have to squeeze till they popped right out.

And she held that thought, feeling good and bad the way it felt good and bad behind the door of the sacristy – except that now, *she* was the powerful one. She could be a good god, like Anne Marie's – the God of girls who are not invited to confess in the sacristy, God of all things bright and beautiful. Or she could cause pain and slaughter, be God of the Massacre of the Innocents.

She remained poised between the two, weighing up her power to act either way, until the hamster gave no more than a sporadic flicker of movement, like the faltering leaps from a dying flame.

Sirens sounded inside Emma's skull. A voice screamed, 'Save him!' Or, 'Save me!' She couldn't make it out, with the sound so loud, so close. She knew the voice, though: it was her own, the one she heard screaming silently behind the sacristy door.

The handle turned.

Anne Marie entered, all happy bluster.

In three skips she was at Emma's side, with the exercise ball in hand.

Emma looked down at Goldie and saw that her grip had loosened. The hamster sat, blinking with astonishment, its silky fur spiked with sweat. Emma stroked smooth the rills of fur, and her breathing slowed. Her chest was light and tight, like after tears.

Anne Marie's hand helicoptered in, lifted Goldie, and deposited him in the exercise ball. Emma watched as this benevolent god closed the ball and set it down gently. With her fingertips, Anne Marie gave the ball a starter-shove. The hamster's feet whirred and he was propelled forward, protected by a bubble that he probably didn't even know was there.

'Did you like it?' said Anne Marie.

Three Weddings

'So that's our new cousin,' I say.

From a safe distance by the drinks table, my sister Caz and I stare at the baby: a great cream puff of a thing. Puzzling over the weirdness of a two-decades-plus age gap, I take in an Eton Mess of frothy white lace and rose-petal skin, fleshy pink feet bursting out of pearl-buttoned soft leather shoes, arms fat-banded at wrist and elbow, and downy hair garnished with a diamante barrette – of all things. Knocking back a glass of lukewarm white, I say, 'Dressed like that, anyone would think it was the baby getting married, not her brother.'

'Half-brother,' Caz corrects, but the point stands, which maybe makes us both uncomfortable. We look to my niece, Charlotte, a proper baby: shoeless, dribble-bibbed and Babygro-ed. I give Charlotte my finger, which she clasps forcefully and plunges into her gummy mouth.

Dad's brother Henry sits at the top table, showing off his baby to Mum. He has that look. Not the brow-low hero-face he used to wear when he'd turn up uninvited after Dad died, to wring the cork from whatever cheap bottle he'd brought or to battle imaginary evils, with stern advice such as, 'Check your tyres – low pressure can be lethal!' and 'Prune back that rosemary, otherwise it will take over the garden!'

No, the other look. The one he had when he showed off his CD player – it was the first I'd seen, but still, I wasn't *that* impressed. Even before Dad died, we were closer to the bevy of females that made up Mum's family; our hard currency took the form of helping hands, homemade cake, and handbags. It baffled me that while Uncle Henry's novelty tech was clearly no better than Dad's records, and even though our smallest girl-cousin was considered hardy enough to take the words 'go away, you're annoying', Henry was somehow so vulnerable that we were expected to stand there feigning interest while his dainty fingers worked the knobs and switches of his 'control panel'.

Yes, it's definitely that look. Same as when he'd call in that bloody great dog he had – a wolfhound, which would come loping to his side, dwarfing him. Same as when he'd talk about whichever pointlessly fast car he'd got or was about to get, leaving pauses only for verbal applause.

I turn to Henry's new wife, wondering how she copes. She sits to his left, eyes lowered, hands in lap like a well-behaved child. It occurs to me that when Henry introduced her, shortly after his first wife cut her hair and left, it was all very seemly. He showed no immoderate pride then – no trace of that look.

'How's Uncle Henry's ex?' I ask.

My sister nods to the French windows, where my uncle's ex-wife holds court. Her short hair is newly dark, and she is talking intensely with mouth and hands. She looks good. Better than I remember – more alive.

'Purple suits her,' I say.

I can't help but turn back to study the new wife, with her high collar and neutral colours. Despite her proximity to Uncle Henry, she seems strangely distant from his baby-bouncing.

Caz's eyes follow mine.

'When I was talking to them earlier, *he* told *her* it was time to nurse the baby,' says Caz. She heaves Charlotte on to her hip as if hoisting a flag – declaring some kind of turf war, which I don't fully get, but kind of do – enough to know which side I'm on. When Caz leans in, so do I.

'Know what else is weird? They're calling the baby Galatea.'

'Galawhat?'

'I know,' she says, eyes rolling. 'It means milk white, apparently. Or fair. It was the name of an artwork that gave its sculptor the hots. Also the name of some nymph, I think.'

I'm about to say, 'Did the nymph do anything cool?' but my uncle turns his daughter towards him, bounces her high, and his face lights – and I mean, *lights* up. With... love, I guess. Although... Where've I seen *that* look before? My mind does a flying-carpet tour of all the churches and art galleries I've ever visited – a visual inventory of saintly eyes rolled heavenward in ecstasy and courtly lovers gazing up at their queens. It comes to me, but it's Caz who puts a word on it.

'He just *adores* her, doesn't he?'

The baby's powder-puff hair, the frilled pouffe of her bottom, and the many-layered ruffles of her skirts flounce up-down, up-down, up-down while Uncle Henry gazes all the while into the eyes of his darling girl.

'Caz,' I say.

'Uh-uh?' She holds a dummy between her teeth while mopping Charlotte's dribble with a napkin.

'I'm having a sexy knickers day.'

'Uh?' Caz chin-raises the dummy, which I take to allow her to speak. 'Sexy knickers?' she says.

'Yeah – but check it out,' I nod towards Galatea. 'There's more lace on that baby's bottom than on mine. Is that normal?'

*

It's Caz who opens the door to Uncle Henry and his gang, so the first I see of Galatea is this little lady – all of seven years old – in the sitting room doorway. Blonde hair tightly tressed. A trench coat belted just so. One knee flexed like she's a contestant for Miss World. And a clutch bag. Seriously. She's so sophisticated, it takes me a moment to find my kiddie voice.

'You must be Galatea!' I serve the words with an extra dollop of enthusiasm, to smother my prickling conscience; since moving abroad, I've made no effort to keep in touch. Uncle Henry – now silvering at the temples – appears behind his daughter. His tiny hands clasp Galatea's shoulders, holding her lightly but surely, as if displaying a garment too precious for anything but the most careful handling. His wife hovers behind them both, like a shop assistant who's not sure she's needed.

'Sorry about the jim-jams,' I say, dispensing protocol kisses. 'I'll put my wedding dress on at the last minute.' Something like shame or embarrassment pinches Uncle Henry's face. Whatever it is, it's contagious. A doubt rips through me; perhaps I should be ready, like the women in films who wake with hair done and make-up fresh? I look to Caz for reassurance and find it in her comfy shirt. Then I look at Charlotte, unselfconsciously sporting her bridesmaid hairdo and a vest – beautiful Charlie, with her smart tights already bagged at the knees and the crotch sagged to a webbed parabola between her thighs. I find us just fine.

'Galatea's ready for her big day!' announces Uncle Henry.

That look: CD players, too-big dogs, shiny fast cars.

My cue to ooh and aah at his daughter.

I won't. Nor will I hit him and ask what he's compensating for. Instead, I take a side-swipe at Mum.

'It's not a big day,' I call out. 'Right, Mum? Like I keep saying, it's not a wedding: I'm just getting married.'

'Oh dear. Yes, darling. I do know,' says Mum, making her way downstairs. Maddening, lovely Mum, who I shooed away but am now so glad to see – already sporting her patient face, ready for Uncle Henry. She'll take him to the kitchen and keep him quiet with tea and cake.

'And you Charlotte?' says Uncle Henry to my niece.

'Charlie,' she says.

'Are you excited about being a bridesmaid?'

Charlie shrugs. She remains hunched over the swell of her breakfast-milk belly, her legs spread wide like no one ever told her not to. But it's her grumpy face and growliness I love most. 'Not a *maid*,' she says. 'I just have to hold flowers.' She turns back to her Lego, but not before giving Galatea the kind of stare Eastwood served up in *Unforgiven*. Galatea blinks her blue eyes, swivels on one of her sparkly sandals and looks to her dad.

'Well!' says Uncle Henry. A nervous laugh. 'Galatea's been getting ready *all* night!'

I'm about to explain how there's no preparation needed. How I've been through everything with Mum, a million times: Caz is here to help with hair and make-up, then we'll rock up at the registry office, do the deed, and be home in time for high tea, with pink champagne and ice cream.

But Uncle Henry gets in first – explains about Galatea's hair. How he plaited it tight especially. 'The secret is to plait the hair when it's damp, and leave it overnight,' he says to Caz, who is standing comb at the ready, poised to coax my curls into an up-do.

'Henry, shall we leave the girls to it?' says Mum.

'Wait till you see this!' says Uncle Henry, as if addressing Wembley Stadium.

One by one, he removes the pins from Galatea's hair, un-coils her blonde bun, loosens the plait, runs his fingers through the length of her hair. And through. And through. With such eagerness and satisfaction. I feel I'm intruding on something best left hidden.

'There!' he says at last. 'A river of gold!'

Charlotte's nostril twitches in contempt. Caz's lips purse. Mum nods fast as if to crank up a polite response. Uncle Henry's wife looks all about like a cornered sparrow. Only Galatea seems comfortable. Wearing a placid smile, she could be a marble maid in the cool, hushed halls of a museum.

It's Caz who first finds her tongue. Pushing up her sleeves she says, 'We've agreed on loose up-dos all round.' Uncle Henry opens his mouth, but Caz turns from him to me. 'We'll have that up, won't we?'

'Tea?' says Mum, shepherding Henry and his wife from the room. He leaves eyes-last, gazing after Galatea till the door closes.

There's a moment of silence then, as there can be when a crowd of gallery-goers are faced with a puzzling artwork.

'Shall we get going?' Caz says to Galatea, taking a brush to her. Galatea accepts the grooming too easily. There's no cross face, no head yanking, no 'ow!'

Charlotte looks on as if presented with a plate of greens.

'How about a game later?' I say. 'Galatea, what do you like to play?'

'I don't play much.' She speaks with a ladylike confidence I never learned to fake, let alone feel. 'I have breakfast club weekdays, then school, homework on Wednesdays, but on the other days I have singing and ballet…' She goes on, talking like a classy weather presenter or a news anchor. Yes, exactly like that: as if reading with studied composure from a prompt.

Galatea begins reciting things she's good at: 'I'm best in class for speech and drama, best in French, nearly best in English, and by far the best at singing...'

'And bragging?' I cut in. It comes out just like that – a hammer blow on the face of a china doll. Charlie bursts into a hyena laugh. Caz gives me a 'really?' stare.

What possessed me to say that?

My guilty brain rustles up words I'll later serve to Caz by way of excuse: 'It was for her own good. If it doesn't come from family, it will come from some kid in the playground.' As for the bullying joy I felt at taking her down a peg – unspeakable. I do my best to bury it. But there's no burying the sudden urge to revolt that I'd felt: the violent refusal of this perfect little creature – or rather the perfecting of this little creature. This creature who should be allowed to just *be*. Herself.

That's what she needs to know.

She stands absolutely still with her blue eyes popping as if she'd been awakened with a slap, and didn't dare move. A blush blooms pink on her porcelain skin. Now is the moment. Now, before she recomposes herself – or is recomposed. I'll explain that she's a fine female even without the flounce and baubles – that she doesn't need to be someone else's idea of perfect.

'Galatea, what I meant to say –'

Henry enters.

'Galatea?' he says, with a what-have-I-got-for-you? From behind his back he produces a small pink vanity case, which Galatea recognises with a smile. My first thought is that the case must contain make-up. I'm about to protest, when Henry lifts the lid to reveal a constellation of sparkly barrettes and swirling satin rainbows of ribbons. 'Enough!' I almost say, but Henry's look of earnestness gives me pause. He selects a strand of blue and draws it from the case slowly, deliberately, as if performing sacred rites or an act of devotion. I sense some sort of violation or violence to come, feel I should intervene – say or do something. But since I don't know what or why, since my feelings are entirely irrational, I simply watch as Henry tilts Galatea's head forward and pulls her hair aside, exposing her vulnerable little nape. Then he ties the ribbon round her neck, and knots it at the back like a choker.

*

'I need you up front with Charlie, herding guests,' Caz says. 'Go on. I'll be fine. Second time around, remember? I won't get lost on my way up the aisle.'

I tug at Caz's collar, bringing it up round her neck to ward off the chill.

'You should have gone for a veil,' I say. 'It would've kept you warmer.'

Caz giggles. A sound so familiar, coming as it does at least weekly by phone. The faint etching on her skin is less so; living abroad, I see Caz too rarely not to marvel that her laugh now echoes in little lines around her face.

'You look beautiful, Caz. Really beautiful.'

'Go!' she says, moist-eyed. 'My nose is already running. I don't need eyes to match. Shoo.'

I unlatch the side-room door and tiptoe across the back of the church as if God were a grumpy neighbour likely to be offended by the clip-clop of my heels. With the cavernous cold of the church, the rows of heads and hats in the pews are topped by cumulus clouds of white breath. In the porch I huddle close to Charlie, who is holding the fort with hearty welcomes and pleased-to-see-yous. Beyond the porch: a gravel-encrusted mud path, leading into grey gusts of horizontal wind and hail.

'Glad I opted for two pairs of tights,' Charlie whispers in my ear between a kiss for Great-aunt Mildred and handshakes for two people I don't know.

'Glad I opted for thermals.'

'Sex-*y*,' Charlie sing-songs, leaning into my neck and puffing so much laughter into my scarf that it comes spouting out of my mouth.

At the end of the path, a scattering of guests emerges from the weather, their hats clamped down with gloved hands, finery flying out like bunting in a storm. Straggling at the back: a curious group of three.

'Oh no,' says Charlie. 'It's *her*.'

I know who, from the tone. Tales of Galatea are a staple gossip feed in family phone calls. There was an Easter when Henry turned up with a video of Galatea's overly apt performance as Eliza Doolittle, insisting that Mum, Caz and Charlie watch from beginning to end ('The longest two hours of my life, including labour,' said Mum). There was a summer get-together where Uncle Henry explained how wrong a modelling agency had been to refuse Galatea on their books ('But anyone can see she's a short-arse,' said Charlie). Then there was the New Year when Galatea turned up with midriff bare and the rest skin-tight ('Why so sexy for family lunch?' said Caz).

'Charlie, why don't you make a break for it?' I say. 'Go and keep Granny company – check she's warm enough.'

Charlie answers with a kiss, and I'm left in charge of how-do-you-dos and lovely-that-you-could-make-its.

I keep one eye on the approach of Uncle Henry. He is silver haired now, slightly stooped, and so much smaller than I remember that my ribcage lifts, visited by an unexpected little throb of tenderness. The cowed figure a step or two behind Henry must be his poor wife – no change there. The figure in front can only be Galatea – wearing a neat leather jacket, a baby-blue lace dress and skin-coloured heels. Perfect for a hip summer wedding. Or if we lived in a magazine. As it is, she looks too right and plain wrong. Like a Botticelli Venus in a cow field.

She expertly picks her way along the path in her stilettos, Henry trotting alongside as if trying to keep up.

When they reach the porch, Galatea resmooths her salon-straightened locks. I get a proper look at her face – an overworked mouth, a chalky mask of powder and foundation, and a smile that doesn't reach her mascara-caked eyes. The sight so saddens me I want to apologise or sympathise, or something, but instead, we share automaton kisses and scant verbal preliminaries before Uncle Henry says, 'What do you think of Galatea's style?'

For the first time I find myself feeling sorry for him. There's something boyish in his face – so keen, so expectant, and yet so sure of adoration for his daughter that he already wears a smile of delight. It's as if the old man he's becoming affords a glimpse of the child he once was. I find myself wondering how he ever survived the luxury borstal that was his and Dad's single-sex public school.

'Her style's... marvellous!'

I search Galatea's eyes to see how this falls. Nothing. I might be gazing at glass.

'She got the outfit together herself,' says Henry, nudging Galatea as if for confirmation or approval. Galatea presents a cold shoulder. Ignores him utterly – a proper little statue. Meanwhile the mother stands by, spare.

'Teenagers, eh?' I say – a verbal fig leaf.

Modesty or mendaciousness bows my head, hiding a whirl of thoughts and emotions within. I wonder if Henry so looked up to his daughter that she now looks down on him. If the mother should have claimed her proper place, so Galatea could claim her own. Or if Galatea caught something of my scorn.

What if ice-chips of the heart are catching?

The question is carried on such cold currents that I strain to see what might lurk beneath. Peering into the murk, I see Henry investing in all that he wasn't allowed to be: dainty, decorative, fragile… Behind his big-man act, the weakness that he was denied. Then, slithering across my consciousness, comes the dark shadow of something ugly – a question: was it weakness, that most universal of human characteristics, that I found so unforgivable, or rather, the idea of a weak *man*?

I look up. See Galatea.

My gaze scales her heels, the stiff folds of her skirt, the jacket that should be a coat, the curtain of hair, and then slips back down to those legs – not dressed in nude-look tights as I had thought, but fashionably bare. Quite bare. In this weather. Galatea's poor, cold-pimpled legs somehow seem to be proof, accusation and hope all at once. With a shudder I am reminded: no one's made of marble. I breathe in, feeling a flicker of hope dancing weakly. Perhaps rebellion is Galatea's escape plan – a way into her own skin.

'Shall we get in out of the cold?' I say.

We shuffle towards the threshold, Henry squeezing his gloved hands, wringing out the chill, while his wife cups hers and puffs white clouds of air into them. Galatea denies herself any arm-hugging or foot-stamping, but holds her jaw too tightly closed; her teeth would chatter if she let them.

I tug at my scarf, making a business of it. Bobbled and lint-laden, it is hardly this season's must-have, but I'm still unwilling to shed it. Uncle Henry, his wife and Galatea watch, curious. If it were just the cold, I'd whip the thing off fast, but as the icy air jabs between the blanket-like coils, it's their gaze that I feel the most; I loosen the wool spirals slowly, feeling all the vulnerability of a change in attitude. Even when the thin skin of my throat is exposed, my hand moves less quickly than it might, stalling as I second-guess whether I dare offer the scarf to Galatea.

Then I too am standing there, looking on curious, now at my own outstretched arm. The question shifts, and I turn my attention to Galatea. I look into her eyes and wait to see whether she too will dare reach out, take the scarf, and wrap it round her neck.

Compassion

My toddler Jon holds me by my hair, yanking hard, and my daughter Debs hangs off my wrist, working my arm like pizza dough. The balls of my feet burn from taking our combined weight, but if I take any support from my heels, it will drive my 'good' sandals into the mud and we'll end up like those prehistoric animals that Debs so loves to hear about – the ones mired in the La Brea tar pits. Tilting my head back to keep my mouth above the fray, I say, 'A *classic* country wedding!' as breezily as I can.

Aunty J beams. She moves a chocolate-dipped strawberry away from her mouth to say, 'We've got it spot on, haven't we?'

I take in the mud-smeared candy stripes of the marquee, the withered corpses of balloons littering the lawn, the lost napkins flapping like wounded birds.

'Spot on!' I say, paraphrasing – a technique we use at work, to help residents feel heard. I try to remember when I last had a conversation that didn't feel like professional protocol.

Jon hammers a fistful of my hair into my skull. Debs works my arm-dough two-handed. I smile out from the grabby heart of the scrummage.

'There's *nothing* so English as a country wedding, is there?'

says Aunty J. Her tone is syrupy, like when she'd present Granny with the latest Laura Ashley catalogue, or return from two weeks' holiday boasting hair sun-bleached blonder than her sister Lisa's. Since both Granny and Aunt Lisa are dead, I'm not sure why we're doing this.

'Don't you think?' says Aunty J.

I don't.

I *do* think that this event is a monumental exercise in approval-seeking and point-scoring. Also, that history didn't just disappear when Granny changed name and nose to become 'Inglish'. And that when Aunty J and Aunt Lisa divvied up the family's meagre supply of blonde genes, Mum somehow became the repository of everything everyone else was trying to shrug off – a role passed to me, since Mum got Alzheimer's. And what with Jon scalping me slowly and Debs fraying my tendons with her swinging, I haven't got the energy to support family games of make-believe.

I breathe in, ready to open a valve on a broiling chestful of home truths.

'Especially when the bride's half Jewish,' I don't say.

I bite my tongue. Just in time. Thank God.

Irritability is one of the symptoms.

'Oh, yes!' I *do* say, which proves I'm fine.

Aunty J's face lights up.

It's fatigue. Straight fatigue – normal, after the past week.

A long-stay resident passed away. After the family had come for her jewellery, photos and knick-knacks, and the end-less forms had been filled, there was still so much unclaimed baggage I didn't know where to put. Like the way she kept her patent leather handbag for 'best', for example, and how, with her dementia, the bleeding from her cancer didn't scare her because she thought she had her period. When I helped her on to the commode, she'd lean in sweetly to confide that she was 'indisposed'. And she would buzz for the toilet, just to get company. One nightshift, while on the 'throne', she reminisced about nursing her baby boy at dawn. I turned off the strip lighting, letting the pale morning light fill the room. We shared a strange nativity: her, her younger self, the memory of her newborn, and me. I couldn't tell the son, of course. Couldn't say, 'Where were you when she felt lonely?' You say, 'I'm sorry for your loss.' Over and over, with each resident that passes, that's what you say.

'Planning was a *nightmare*,' says Aunty J, raising her eyes to the heavens, as if this might be God's fault. 'Never again!'

'Poor you!' I say – *proof again that I'm fine*.

Although I'm not sure I said it with feeling. My mind's elsewhere. I'm thinking about sanitary pads. The brand Whisper Soft, to be precise. I'd just changed for the last time the pad of the lady that died, when I noticed the branding, and that's what got me going with the psychotherapist.

'Why "*Whisper* Soft"?' I said.

He looked at me like I was something in a Petri dish. It made everything worse, that sterile office, where professional standards and secrecy keep everything clean and controlled.

'It's because there are things people don't want to acknowledge,' I said. 'They'd rather pretend they're not there. And they *can*,' I said, 'because there's *someone* else whose job it is to dress sores, mop dribbling mouths, wipe bottoms leaking brown and red –'

'I'll stop you there,' he said. That was when he told me about compassion fatigue. It's a thing, apparently. Symptoms can include irritability and disproportionate reactions, denial accompanied by cynicism and aggression, and intrusive images of another's trauma.

'Be vigilant,' he told me. 'You're at increased risk, being a carer in your private life too.'

He prescribed starting the day with 'a relaxing ritual'. I didn't ask what that might be, because it didn't sound like anything that would fit with the palaver of keeping an eye on Mum while getting two pre-schoolers up – and because I'm fine.

Except that I'm eating my hair, thanks to Jon, and my new cardi will wear thin with Debs' swinging.

'Careful, love,' I say. 'I want that to last.'

'You know Maya's here?' says Aunty J.

'*Is* she?' Maya's the last thing I need. My voice comes out too much like the one I use to praise Jon's Play-Doh and Debs' pasta collages, or Kevyn, when he's managed to get himself to the doctor. I cough, moderate it, try again. 'How *lovely*!'

'How long's it been?' says Aunty J.

Not long enough, I think, because there's no getting away from Maya – every scrap of her news is passed round the family like titbits about celebrities. Come back from a double shift and you get Mum or Aunty J filling you in on Maya's rise from PA to boss. Do Kevyn's benefit claim and it's Maya's surgeon husband. Contain your kid's temper tantrum and you get to hear how Maya's newborn is sleeping nights. Now Mum's got Alzheimer's, I hear Maya stories on a loop. And yet Maya legged it to London as soon as she could. Disappeared as suddenly as her mother – not as tragically, thank God, but almost as definitively. Didn't call when Mum was diagnosed, though I know from Aunty J that she'd been told. Didn't come to Granny's funeral, let alone help with the arrangements. 'Couldn't face it', apparently. *What had it been? Twenty years?*

'You *must* see her,' says Aunty J. 'I'll get her.'

'Don't!' I say. It just slips out. Aunty J does a double-take, and forgets to sip from the champagne flute she's raised to her mouth. I mop up the verbal spillage as best I can, saying, 'Please stop that swinging, Debs. I won't tell you again.'

Then there she is, like an apparition: Maya – just beyond the marquee. So much like her mother it's unsettling. Same baby-doll nose, same swishy blonde hair. So much like herself too, despite the years, though she's lost the stunned dreaminess she had after her mother's accident. She's dressed all in pale blues and whites, clean and fresh. Even her shoes. She's grown tall, unweighted. I watch her bend gently as a reed in a breeze towards a little one, also dressed in blues and whites – *her daughter, must be – so much like her and Aunt Lisa* – a sweet moppet, proffering a posy.

The scrum senses a change in the emotional temperature. Debs lets my cardi slacken. Jon loosens his grip on my hair. Aunty J follows my gaze.

'Maya's the *spit* of Aunt Lisa,' I say, without thinking.

I could kick myself. It's not like me to be insensitive. I would kick myself, if I wasn't so bogged down in the mud. Aunt Lisa was Aunty J's sister, after all.

'Mummy, who's that?' says Debs.

'One second, Debs,' I say, taking Aunty J's emotional pulse by checking her face. No, we're all right: Aunty J's troubled, but not for herself. She leans towards me, her face serious.

'Mummy, who's that?'

'Debs, one second.'

'You know…' says Aunty J.

Here we go – something else to know and not say.

'… She remembers nothing – about Lisa.'

'Nothing?' I say, because it was supposed to be temporary: 'temporary amnesia', the doctors said – an extreme reaction to the trauma of the accident. That was two decades ago; time enough, you'd think.

'Mummy, who's that?' Debs shakes my arm.

'I rang Uncle Ben to invite him – for Maya's sake. That's when he told me: Maya never recovered any memories of her mother – can't even remember Li's face. I can't believe Ben didn't tell us. He *should* have told us…' Aunty J is glossy-eyed.

I touch her arm, shake my head in sympathy.

But I can't help thinking how strange this is, because Aunt Lisa's a regular visitor to my head. She comes in brisk and breezy, giving advice, or going on about her projects. Sometimes she's with little Maya, sometimes without – almost always without Uncle Ben – an absence that I notice but, as in life, don't mention. Sometimes, Aunt Lisa takes tea with Granny, Mum and Aunty J.

Most often though, I see her drowning.

I have ever since Mum told me what happened. Sometimes I see Mum too, trying to find a dry place on her tissue and saying, 'Maya was there for hours before they found her. Just standing, petrified.' But mostly, I see Aunt Lisa. The images unreeled in my mind as Mum spoke, and horror set them on automatic rerun, so I have a visual memory of something I never saw. Except that I have seen it – do see it. Very often, these last few weeks, come to think of it. Even in sleep: I dream that I'm stuck in a body unable to scream.

'You won't mention Lisa, will you?' says Aunty J. Before I can answer, she says, 'I mean, I *know* you won't.'

'Mummy. Mummy. Mummy,' says Debs.

'She's done *so* well, considering,' says Aunty J. 'So sensitive, poor thing. Always was. Born with a skin too few…'

That gets me bristling. 'Not like some of us with a tough old hide, eh?' I want to say, but Debs interrupts. The words remain lodged in the back of my throat, like a barb.

*

Mum sits at the far end of the table, with teapot and biscuits, ready to serve. Aunt Lisa's claimed the rest of the kitchen for our science experiment – though it's hers really, to do with her teacher training.

I stand by the table, where I've been posted, despite earlier pleading with Mum: 'Maya could watch instead of me; it doesn't matter if she's not the right age group.' My objections still buzz inside me like trapped bluebottles, bumping up against the lid of Mum's tensely whispered last words on the matter: 'Do it for Aunt Lisa.'

So now Aunt Lisa's turning the kitchen into a science lab. She removes beakers and a flask from a cardboard box, moving quickly, confidently, as if nothing in this world ever got broken. Mum glances from broom cupboard to sink, and I know she has already mentally sought out a cloth, dustpan and brush, in case. Standing between them, Aunt Lisa so keen and carefree, Mum all smiling attentiveness, it occurs to me that there can't be one without the other – they're like players on a see-saw. I wonder if this is always the way: if something divides listeners and talkers, givers and takers, losers and winners.

'I have been put here to listen,' I think, the words sinking slowly from mind to belly.

'This teacher training is about getting my life back,' says Aunt Lisa. She says it gung-ho, with a flick of her hair. Mum nods, heavy-headed, purse-lipped, which means this has something to do with Aunt Lisa leaving Uncle Ben.

The divorce is something Mum has told me not to talk about: 'Keep it here,' she said, tapping her chest to mean her heart – my heart. 'For Maya's sake.'

I turn to Maya, wondering how much she knows. She sits

111

by the Aga, dressing her doll's white-gold hair. Maya's eyes are round and clear, untroubled, even by the alarming porcelain-skinned perfection of her doll – a doll that I helped choose. For one sparkling second, when Mum placed that doll in my hands and asked if I liked it, it had been mine. But even before she explained that Maya needed our support, that the doll would be a gift, it felt like a borrowed dream. I was so aware that its perfection was unsustainable, that the doll would be eroded by accident or rough handling; I was relieved to put it back behind the protective film of its box.

Watching Maya play, I see that the doll could only be hers; it might have been made in her image. 'Genes' is how Mum explains this physiological gulf: 'Some people get lucky.' She jokes that she got Granny's old nose, Aunt Lisa got Granny's new nose, and Aunty J got something in-between. I once said, 'So Aunt Lisa got more luck than genes then,' but Mum got her serious face and said, 'You have a fine nose. Never forget. It's who we are – where we're from.' This too is something I mustn't talk about. 'For Granny's sake,' says Mum. 'Keep it here,' she says, tapping her chest.

'I feel like a cork bobbing up in water,' says Aunt Lisa, turning the tap on full, to fill the flask. Turning to me, she says, 'Heads up!' She places on the table a Frankenstein's monster of an object: a double-spouted vase with one normal spout and, on the other side, a helter-skelter spout. 'Communicating vessel!' proclaims Aunt Lisa.

'Isn't this exciting!' says Mum, giving me a look.

'Yes!' I say, with as much pep as I can.

Maya wanders over, followed by their old red setter, Murphy. She peers at the vase, while the dog noses the table. I gently shove his greying muzzle aside to make room for Maya, but she turns away from the table to examine me instead –

a direct, unembarrassed appraisal. Then she looks back at the vase, before examining me again. 'It's like you,' she says, pointing at the helter-skelter spout. She points at my hair and makes a curliewurlie gesture with her finger. After studying me a moment longer, she adds, 'Your nose isn't straight either.'

I *want* to hate her, but her eyes shine with guiltless curiosity. I see no trace of malice, nor even the kindness that lit Granny's eyes when she offered to help get my nose 'fixed', explaining in her German accent: 'Eats better fur sinks to fit in.' In her innocence, Maya doesn't seem to have noticed that, in contrast to Mum and me, she and Aunt Lisa are more like the clean, straight spout on the right – everything you might desire in a spout.

'Ready?' says Aunt Lisa. Her voice is tigerish, like someone who's only ever ready. Like the girls who get picked first for netball.

'Yep!' I say – my best imitation of someone who knows how to catch.

Clinging to the table edge by her fingertips, Maya rises shakily on tiptoes. Her mouth drops so far open, anything might blow in there. Her blue eyes take in everything, unfiltered even by a blink. She seems so wide open to the world that I find myself thinking of that doll and the box that seemed not just desirable, but necessary. I make struts of my hands, reach under her arms, prop her up.

Aunt Lisa pours water into the double-spouted vase. It fills, helter-skelter spout and all, until every part is equally full. Maya wriggles, turns, looks at me – my hair, my nose. That same curiosity. I take in her translucent skin, her glass-smooth hair, her sky-blue eyes, and feel a jab of spite. I want to tell her of the suffering levied on beauties in fairy tales – spindles, poison apples, black-magic sleep...

113

But Maya reaches for my hand, as naturally as if she were scratching her nose or flicking the hair from her face. I look down and she looks up, trusting as a kitten; I can't help opening my heart to her. I hold her hand in mine, and she leans into me.

'There's more!' says Aunt Lisa. That netball-team voice again.

She takes two identical beakers and fills one with water. Into it she places a double-jointed straw. Nothing happens. I fear a fail, for one stomach-shrivelling instant. But undaunted, Aunt Lisa taps the straw. Slowly, steadily, almost stealthily, water creeps up, across, down into the empty beaker. By the end of the experiment, both beakers stand exactly half-full.

'Amazing, Li!' says Mum.

'Amazing!' I say on cue, but my voice doesn't come out right. I add more life, more lift and say again, 'A*ma*zing!'

'Questions?' says Aunt Lisa.

I dredge my mind. The questions are there; I feel them thrashing in the eddy and swirl of my emotions. There's the shadow of something about Uncle Ben and divorce. Something about Jewishness, and how some members of our family get to shrug it off like old clothes, while others have to pick it up and keep it carefully – but *quietly* too. Then there's something about this idea that some are born to support, while others shine. But there's nothing I can cajole into a sentence, and this isn't the time or place anyway; I contain the churn and swill behind a shrug, a smile.

'The question *is*,' says Aunt Lisa, 'how the water gets from one beaker to the other.'

'Yeah!' I say – then actually think, because if the beakers can share their load despite their separate glass skins, we might do the same in our family: even things out, say between Mum and Lisa, or Maya and me. But I can take the thought no further; Mum prompts me with a look.

'That's so cool,' I say. 'You're the best, Aunt Lisa!'

*

Like an apparition, Maya floats across the lawn towards us. I'm seized by a panic that's got the primal grip of a struggle for survival.

Disproportionate reaction, I think, but that doesn't stop me telling Aunty J that I'll be right back, and dashing to where Kevyn's sitting hunched over a Pimm's – *not great, with the antidepressants.*

'Here,' I say, settling Jon in Kevyn's lap.

'Stay with Daddy,' I say to Debs.

Kevyn raises his hands, pleading. I almost say 'Chrissake,' but I know he's having a bad day. How could I *not* know with all the pre-event coaxing needed to get him here?

'For a second?' I say. 'Can you? *Please?*'

I'm stumbling back to Aunty J in my stupid sandals when she leads the moppet-poppet away. Maya does a smiling finger-wave to her daughter, then turns to face me.

That's when Aunt Lisa turns up, wearing the same clothes she wore in my mind the day Mum told me about the accident. She strides into my head, leading a little Maya by the hand.

They walk along the river, which is swollen. Its surface rucks and puckers but is otherwise still, apart from the dog's splashing. I see Murphy swimming, then ceasing to make headway, not far from the bank. He paddles on the spot – fast, and faster, but the splashing grows less, as if the water's being dragged down as fast as it's churned up. The dog's eyes widen to the whites. He makes as if to yelp, but before he can, the river swallows him.

On the bank, Maya shouts, 'Mummy, Murphy!'

I see Aunt Lisa run to the river, her hair swishing, the lead swinging dogless in her hand. She skids, slides down the bank. The dog resurfaces: up and then down, as if the water's playing peek-a-boo.

Aunt Lisa wades in, shin-high. She looks about, but sees no trace of the dog. No trace of anything, in the murk – but if she can get to where he resurfaced – a couple of strokes from the bank… She wades out. Water spills, sluggish but determined, over the top of her wellies.

'Stay there,' she says to Maya. Soaked to the knee, Aunt Lisa braces herself against the cold, inhales, plunges. She's in.

And under, almost as quick. Like the dog. There, then gone.

The water flows on, untroubled.

*

Someone inside my skull screams and screams. It can't be me because my jaw's clenched so hard, my teeth ache. Also because Maya's standing in front of me, all smiling composure.

'It took me a moment to recognise you,' she says. 'You look… good.'

Last time I caught sight of my reflection, it scared me so much that I brushed my teeth with my eyes closed. I can't imagine I look any better now, but all I say is, 'How are *you*?'

The question comes of its own accord – a professional reflex. It's what we ask residents, to open a window on how they're feeling so we can adapt to their needs. I'm usually ready for whatever might come through that window, but I find myself waiting for Maya's answer shaky-legged, unsure I can take more emotional weight.

'I'm well,' she says.

I scan her face. Not a single worry line. Brow as smooth as a boiled egg. I think of that doll she once had – the perfect skin, eyes like a new sky. I wonder where all that suffering went. It can't have vaporised.

'My daughter,' she says, with a nod in the direction of the moppet-poppet.

'She looks like you.' I dose the words carefully, checking Maya's face for discomfort at the word 'like', coming in fast with 'you' so that 'Aunt Lisa' can't arise as a potential sentence end. Maya gives only a studied smile.

'Where are your two?' she asks.

Before giving a nod in their direction, I check with a corner-eye glance that they're presentable – then mentally ask what sort of mother I am.

'They're beautiful,' says Maya, watching while Debs spits whatever she's been chewing into Kevyn's hand. I almost snap. *Goodness knows, I change enough bedpans while making small talk. Can't we do away with the niceties?* But I see Mum in my mind, tapping her chest. *Keep it in, keep it in.*

'And your husband? What does he do?' asks Maya.

'He doesn't – at the moment. Sick leave.' You can't be on leave if you're unemployed, but it seems kinder not to say. A white lie – a small thing, but it weighs heavy, with the rest. I feel myself sinking into the mud again, and imagine how much lighter I'd be if I could let out everything that mustn't be said. It'd be like taking off my shoes after a long shift. First the swell, fiercer than before, then the plumped flesh gradually easing, draining, and the relief, the *blessed* relief.

'And you're a nurse?' she says, studying my hands, which are red and raw from scrubbing. I notice her fingers curled around her champagne flute, the pink and white ovals of her fingernails.

'Care work,' I say.

'So important,' she says, with the polite interest of a royal on a walkabout.

'Not so important that you'd do it,' is what comes to mind – to my mouth – to the tip of my tongue. I press my lips together just in time. *Keep it in, keep it in.*

'And you? PR, isn't it?'

'Not for much longer; I want to give up work.' She talks about selling her company – takeovers, buyouts – making it sound clean and simple, like Aunt Lisa 'getting her life back' after she dumped Uncle Ben. I think how easy it must be to move forward unweighted by memory, relieved even of the suffering of one's younger self.

That's when Aunt Lisa comes to mind again – or rather, her science experiment. I see all the suffering I've ever known, everything everyone would rather forget, turned to water. I imagine siphoning off the overflow, levelling things out, putting Maya's memories back where they belong – and I'd start with Aunt Lisa drowning. I imagine the relief at the weight of the images draining away. 'I remember…' I'd say, and then I'd let the words come slowly, steadily, almost stealthily, creeping from me to Maya, until her pale blue eyes were brimming with cares that were no longer mine.

Then I see that her eyes are already filling. She's looking at me, cautious – but clearly troubled.

'Tell me,' she's saying. 'What's the matter?'

'I'm fine.'

'No, you're not. You're crying.'

It's only then that I feel my cheeks damp, the water leaking from my eyes.

Maya frees her hands of her glass, drops her clutch to the ground.

'Come,' she says, taking my hand as naturally as if it were her own.

'Let it out,' she says, and I lean into her.

Lettre à Simone

Chère Simone,

My latest attempt to write your story is a failure. 'Laboured,' says my editor, capturing in one word all my trying and failing.

This unhappy business started with that photograph by Robert Capa. Given your attempts to escape your past, and the picture's role in making this impossible, I apologise for bringing it up so brutally.

Rest assured, you are safe; nothing more can harm you.

The picture: beneath a *Tricolore* flag hoisted high, a jubilant crowd spills down a paved street – men in grubby shirtsleeves, aproned matrons, children in make-do-and-mend clothes... In the foreground, an elderly man, gaze downcast, carries a bundle of possessions. To your right, my left, four women with their hair in dishevelled victory rolls walk in staggered alignment. A helmeted police agent strides by your side. They turn to you. You present a classical three-quarters profile. Though you are in the first bloom of youth, you wear a housecoat as if snatched from the duties of homemaking. Your head is newly shaved, your temple branded. Yet you step serenely into the foreground. All your attention is dedicated to the sleeping infant cradled in your arms.

'Who is she? What happened?' I wanted to know. The title answered the second question only: *La Tondue de Chartres – Shaved Woman of Chartres*.

A little research yielded your name. The etymology is the Hebrew word for 'to hear'.

Wanting to hear you, I determined to restore your voice. Free-written 'sketches' brought forth a forbidden war-time romance, an illegitimate baby, a vengeful crowd, a cruel comeuppance. You were an unhappy lover, a worthy mother.

An ideal victim.

But no real character; you lacked agency.

I returned to *La Tondue*, equipped with an idea borrowed from art theory: works must present a 'pregnant moment' in which something is about to happen. Short-story writers use a similar technique, starting on the day something different happens, *in media res*; the action makes for choices under pressure which reveal character. The plan was to identify the action and work backwards to find you. But Capa's picture rendered no pregnant moment, only a *fait accompli*. There was no getting you out. You were sealed in. Done.

I tried another theory, more closely related to photography. This one came from Henri Cartier-Bresson, a friend of Capa's: photographs must capture *l'instant décisif*, the decisive moment, where compositional elements come together harmoniously to make a formally perfect image. Capa's composition rivals any Renaissance masterpiece. The feet of the foreground figures trace a triangle that leads the eye into the picture. Like a mandorla or halo, the triangle marks about you a sacred space. The townspeople's gaze converges on you, the focal point, while the buildings in the background trace a parallel perspective, converging on the flag. Everything is exactly in place – not a foot out of line.

It's hard to believe such a composition was seized in haste, *à la sauvette*.

In a shot taken instants before, the flag is misplaced, off-centre. The crowd is more dispersed, so the women to your right stand out as individuals. Their faces speak hilarity, but also shock and confusion. Your mother is by your side, walking in step. You make your way without being manhandled. Your expression is neutral, your head high.

The facts, differently arranged, make a messier truth.

Facts are unimportant, said Cartier-Bresson; the decisive moment is about *order*.

This fact, from an eyewitness account, mattered very much to me: as you walked, you wept.

Did you ever hear of a German Enlightenment thinker called Gotthold Ephraim Lessing? He was devoted to the principle of tolerance, notably for Jews. (Also, the idea that I mentioned earlier of the pregnant moment.) According to Lessing, in the plastic arts, pain must be conveyed through beauty. Without beauty, there can be no pity, only repugnance.

Perhaps Capa was right not to speak your pain?

Evocation is what Cartier-Bresson prescribed, in place of facts.

In *La Tondue*, what do you evoke? Your sweet maternal embrace sends the viewer's gaze looping in a tender figure of eight, from mother to child, for infinity; you could be Raphael's tondo *Madonna della Sedia*. Do you see it? The ultimate female role model, according to the Catholic religion in which we were raised.

No further from where I started, I sought traces of your character in other pictures taken that day.

The earliest was from the morning of 16 August 1944. By the *épicerie* on the corner of rue Sainte-Même, you run flat-footed towards the camera, in house slippers. Your housecoat is open, revealing your checked dress and the swell of your nursing-mother's breasts. In the background, a soldier aims at something to your left, my right. Directly behind you runs a figure in the get-up we've come to associate with the Resistance: scruffy jacket, floppy fringe and rifle. He had joined that very morning, as the American tanks rolled in. You had been granted leave to fetch your baby, and he was charged to escort you home and back to the *Préfecture*. Chartres was not yet freed. There was an exchange of gunfire. You dashed for cover.

But the legend of the reproduction said: 'Woman accused of collaboration fleeing humiliation having been shaved'.

This slippage from description to interpretation brought to mind something I learnt from my daughter (a Criminology postgraduate): according to the sociologist Nils Christie, the role of 'ideal victim' is not open to just anybody. We like victims to be weak. Say, a young female. They should be carrying out respectable projects, such as childcare. They must also be some place where they have a perfect right to be – for example, walking down a main street in broad daylight. The terms 'victim' and 'offender' are mutually exclusive; the offender should be big, bad and in no personal relationship to the victim. A jeering crowd of strangers will do. The 'victim' must be able to command enough power to establish identity as an ideal victim, but weak enough to pose no threat to other important interests. A woman conforming to class-based gender expectations does this perfectly.

Another thing my daughter taught me: surveillance is never neutral (Foucault).

You had a camera in your face much of that day. In one picture, you and your mother, scalps naked, crouch on a stone step at the *Préfecture*. Your mother holds your sleeping baby and stares at the camera, accusing. You squint with empty eyes. You seem past caring. About anything. Ever again.

This shot comes after the one at the *épicerie*. You have your baby and the bundle of belongings that turns up in *La Tondue de Chartres* carried by your father. Perhaps you picked up baby and bundle in one swoop. I imagine hasty maternal logistics – the workings of the scrambled but strangely efficient mind of a new mother. I notice that you swapped slippers for more gracious footwear with a bit of heel.

Did you know something about ideal victims?

May I tell you of some beautiful images I found when researching you – thanks to you, in a way? They don't fit here or anywhere that I can see, but I have come to associate them with you. Picture this: a sunlit room, where a young woman with too many teeth smiles candidly from mussed bedsheets. And: a woman washing poselessly at a basin, breasts unconstrained, body hair unchecked, droplets of water tracing her curves. And (my favourite): a smile appearing like a sudden sunrise from a neckline pulled over loose, unbrushed hair. These are from film footage apparently shot without permission as part of an espionage programme executed by German soldiers involved with French women during the war. No matter how hard I try, I cannot sync this knowledge to what I see: women glorying in the luxury of their bodies. Women who, in those moments, felt free.

Did your lawyer explain that there was no law against 'horizontal collaboration'?

Your love life came up a lot at your trial. In the archives, you consistently refer to Erich, the father of your child, as your 'fiancé' – a veil of respectability you wouldn't now need. All the same, workshop feedback made it clear that Erich had to be central to your story. In later drafts, I included that he went missing on the eastern front. Also, that in peace time he had been a shopkeeper, like your father – only a bookseller, not a *crémier* – hence his posting to the *Frontbuchhandlung*, the German military bookshop in Chartres. When reading accounts of your 'easiness', I jotted two words in current usage that might have been useful to you during your interrogation and trial: 'polyamory' and 'slut-shaming'. However, I left out of every draft your *amourettes*. In particular, I neglected to mention that after Erich was posted to the front, you became the mistress of another German soldier, all the while maintaining your long-distance relationship with Erich.

Among items requisitioned from your home were: photographs in which you appear in the company of Germans, in 'suggestive' poses; about two hundred letters, almost all in German; a notebook in German; and a poem, also in German.

Pictures and words.

Which was more incriminating?

It seems that, to correspond uncensored with Erich, you set up an illicit delivery system, reclaiming your full right to a freedom that war had abraded: privacy.

In later life, desperate to be free of your past, you destroyed all personal photographs and documents that might betray your history, even to your and Erich's child.

One thing slipped easily into each version of your story: your *Baccalauréat*, which put you among an elite 5 per cent of females educated to this level in France in 1941. You strove to 'perfect' your German; excellence, apparently, wasn't enough. Why this headlong pursuit of another tongue? What did you hope to leave behind? Or find? Did you sense that your *mère patrie* reserved no easy place for your unwieldy intelligence?

Your dreams and aspirations flowered in doodles scrawled in your schoolbooks, but you eschewed love hearts and initials.

Aged fourteen, you opted instead for swastikas.

You were an ardent Anglophobe, like your mother. She reportedly once spat out of a window, saying, '*Tiens, voilà pour les Anglais.*' In court, she explained that her distinguished military forebears had suffered strife with Perfidious Albion. Was hatred her way of clinging to a nobler past when your family slid from bourgeois to broke? You lived your straitened circumstances as an injustice. Germany promised better: a force to crush the Bolshevik menace and do away with the Freemasons and Jews who held you back, kept you down. You could be free...

A writerly observation: everyone lies – at least occasionally. For a writer seeking to understand character, asking 'if' is therefore not as useful as 'where', 'what' and 'how', which can help resolve the underlying question of 'why'. Lies signpost fears and desires, and the lies we tell ourselves hide truths we cannot, or will not, face.

Facts, differently arranged: by all accounts, your father's *crémerie* failed because your mother was utterly disagreeable; people took their custom elsewhere.

Where most French citizens followed the path of least resistance, you actively collaborated, presenting yourself for recruitment by German administrative services as soon as your exams were over. You wanted your own money. Then better hours, more money. Daughter of a bankrupt, you hustled your way to a better position three times in as many years.

The picture where you look happiest was taken at the *Wehrmacht* headquarters, several months before the *Libération*. In the background is a requisitioned residence with bow windows, balustrades and stately lawns. Before that are ranks of German soldiers and non-commissioned officers, almost identical in uniforms and crew cuts. You stand at the front with eight other secretaries and interpreters, all coiffed, heeled and smartly wrapped in winter coats. A smile chubs your cheeks. You have about you a gaucheness that reminds me how young you were. You look almost too pleased to be huddled, arms linked, in that girly in-group. I think, with a heart twinge, of your description by an ex-classmate – 'thoroughly unpleasant' – and how you were ostracised at school.

Work wasn't all rosy. I read those letters where you complained about conditions and the supervisor who worked less than you and left earlier. Still, standing there with your *Wehrmacht* colleagues, all so keen and alert, you could almost be a corporate line-up. We no longer display female workers up front, like rare birds; however, they are still more likely to be in supporting positions and lower paid. (In corporate communications, we tell a different story, using gender-neutral language and illustrations that demonstrate diversity. Is this a truth-to-come or a lie?)

There's a media-friendly clinical psychologist, in my time, called Jordan Peterson. 'The acceptable face of the alt-right' is how a friend describes him, meaning he is no good thing. I lent him my ear one time, to form an opinion, and thought of you. Not because of your political sympathies, though French politics still comprises a far right. Peterson was talking feminism – an idea that women's opportunities and rights must equal those of men. In discussion of the wage gap between men and women, Peterson stated that on average women are more agreeable, a personality trait associated with lower earning potential, career development and social status. Peterson's solution: coach females to be assertive. What if, though, agreeableness is prevalent among females because society sanctions disagreeableness in this population? Peterson's approach would treat symptom, not cause.

Did being disagreeable do you and your mother any favours? Or were you punished?

*

You got pregnant on labour service in Munich, where you had gone to join Erich, who was recovering from wounds in a military hospital. You surely knew your relationship was forbidden. Did you, as with letter censorship, decide you were an exception to the rule? Or entertain hope that Germany would come to see the special truth of you and welcome you as its own?

When your pregnancy came to light, you were banished; did you then see the lie of Nazism – at least where you were concerned?

I hardly dare think what you knew about the rest.

At the same time, I cannot help but wonder.

There's a picture of you at the *Préfecture*, before the leaded panes of a great window. You stand ranked with twenty-eight others rounded up that day. Nine men are at the front, mostly sitting. The rest, women, stand behind: a gender negative of the picture at the *Wehrmacht* headquarters. The men are distinguished by caps, comb-overs, middle partings and bald patches. The women are mostly shaved. Their shoulders sag and their arms are crossed or hugged about their bodies. In their eyes, there is something defeated, broken. You are the only one with a baby. You are the only one branded – twice.

When that shot was taken, you had been arrested without warrant and punished without charge. You'd had no trial; that came after.

Some believe you were innocent – that it was not you but your friend Ella who denounced those neighbours for listening to English radio, leading to the arrest of five, the deportation of four and the death of two. That would be an easier story to tell. Would it be true?

Your mother was also charged with denunciation. Your father faced the unofficial charge of having been weak, of not having known how to keep his women in check – though he attempted to throttle you when you returned pregnant, and forbade you from giving birth at home.

In the course of our *Libération*, tens of thousands of people all over France suffered a similar ordeal to the one inflicted on you at the *Préfecture*. Almost all were women, mostly working class. One theory is that your humiliation exorcised the shame of a majority that had lain down in the face of an enemy. By seizing your body, demonstrating power over it, men reasserted their position as active dominants. While proceedings varied, there was often recourse to makeshift uniforms or Resistance armbands, a desk manned by an 'official' and the execution of punishments in a public place or civic institution.

A semblance of order.

My editor sent me a link to a literary magazine that refuses to consider stories featuring violence against women. No doubt woman-as-victim is too easy a narrative as my first drafts attest. But what of voicing difficult truths?

What of silence as a means of oppression?

I asked an elderly member of my family what she knew about punishment for horizontal collaboration. In her town, a woman was stripped and marched naked through the streets, then shaved. Did that happen? I asked. My relative supposed it did but knew nothing. Nothing? I said. I had seen a photograph: a scene of such shocking brutality, my eye sought refuge in the dappled bark of the plane trees that punctuated the crowds of onlookers. Nothing, she said, her mouth shrinking small and tight. Nothing at all. No.

After your trial and internment, you tried to disappear: moved, married, had more children. Your past caught you up. Your marriage broke down. You became depressed, alcoholic. Aged 44, in the clinic where you delivered your firstborn, you died.

Many times, when researching, I came upon reproductions of *La Tondue de Chartres* coupled with captions stating that you were being taken to prison. Released from the *Préfecture*, you were actually being escorted, for your own safety, home. Peacetime returned many women to their 'proper' place: housewife, mother, silent beauty – exactly as you were framed by Capa's Contax.

Simone, I have come to accept that I cannot do right by you.

Nor can I put you right.

I am so sorry.

May I offer a parting gift? There's this artist I like called Valentine Fournier, who works with old photographs, typewritten words and tensions that she creates between them. One of her artworks shows a pin-up style nude, posed like a mannequin and shot from behind to give a tantalising glimpse of golden hair and bare bottom. The image is bannered: '*Liberté, mon cul*' – Freedom? My arse…

Bien à vous.

Sonya

PS

My editor read this letter, and wondered if the talk of creative process imposes distance.

How to get closer?

I booked cheap tickets to Chartres.

Then, because my chest was tight in anticipation of pain, a hotel with more stars than my budget allowed.

'The escapade offer,' I confirmed, to a silky-voiced receptionist. 'For two.'

It felt like surfacing for air. Renaissance sumptuary laws, of all things, came spinning through my mind. I sat phone to ear, but in imagination was in the Louvre, reeling before Veronese's

Wedding of Cana. Veronese was the painter who turned Last Suppers and other Biblical scenes into feasts so lavish they caused scandal. Eventually, he had to answer to the Inquisition for indecency – a worrying detail that visits me, and evaporates, whenever I gaze into his skies of lapis blue...

The regional train to Chartres cuts across rich farmlands. They pass in a gold-green blur, interrupted by magpies flapping a piebald landing. I count: one for sorrow, two for joy... Three. *For a girl.*

At Chartres station is a memorial to wartime heroism. Beyond that opens a wide, clean street, edged by buildings of careful proportions. The di-twin towers of the cathedral dominate the townscape. One is Gothic lace, the other smooth-tiled like lizard skin.

On the way to my fancy hotel, I eavesdrop.

'He never managed his money...' says a passer-by.

'He had it coming...' tuts their companion.

I quash the spring in my step, and my thoughts turn to your 'decadent' social engagements. Music on the gramophone, singing. Visiting-gifts of butter and bottles. You, perched on some officer's delighted knees... Pleasures made guiltier by the privations of your compatriots.

What effect, if any, did hardships have on your pleasures?

The hotel reception is dove grey and gold. After check-in, the receptionist presses a tourist map into my hands, promising 'historic and beautiful sights'.

Chartres boasts a rich patrimony – twenty-three sites, accessible by miniature tourist train, and illuminated at night. Street names commemorate the Resistance – Charles de Gaulle, Jean Moulin... You are nowhere mentioned. However, there is a walking route around wash houses where, in days gone by, washerwomen scrubbed the town's dirty laundry clean.

Sipping espresso, I shuffle pictures of you, plotting on the map the sites of your Calvary.

Once outside, my feet resist the route.

'*La ville est trop belle,*' I explain to my companion. Boutiques offer artisanal chocolates, cheeses, and perfect fruits in an artfully distressed dresser. At a baker's, *croquembouche* tower beneath the glassy veneer of an irreproachable glaze. Homeware stores propose dreams of loveliness to townsfolk feathering nests: broad-backed sofas, linen made to last… An antiques store displays an imitation nineteenth-century oil: *Convivial Moment between Persons of Quality*.

At Logis Claude Huve, we pause to admire fluted Corinthian columns. Crammed beneath the cornice, a grotesque grimaces between rosettes and curling acanthus leaves. An inscription asserts: 'Huve built this house to beautify the town and for posterity.'

A beggar with an Old Testament beard squats at the column base, unmoving beside the stream of footfall. He makes a jarring juxtaposition: what is passed on, what is passed by.

I think to give money, but my hand refrains: I cannot graciously retrieve my purse from the jumble in my bag.

We walk on, pass by.

A plaque commemorates a soldier fallen for freedom on 16 August 1944.

Posters welcoming us to Chartres promote its *cadre de vie agréable*. Signs indicate rue du Cheval-Blanc, where Capa took his shot. 'Restaurants!' they say. 'Shops open!'

We take the opposite direction, only to stumble upon the site of the requisitioned shop where you met with Erich. Behind a gracious shopfront, painted *chocolat-praliné*, are ranked pastries and aproned ladies with smiles.

Looking for a place to lunch, we pass the site of your

family's failed business. It is shrouded under Christo-like wraps: 'Refurbishment' announces a sign.

In such a town, you must have everywhere met with painful reminders.

The cathedral chimes.

We lunch on a *terrasse* bathed in afternoon sun.

Our host seats us well, asking our pleasure.

Weaving between tables comes the seller of a charity magazine.

'Not here,' says our host.

My companion and I joke and chatter throughout *entrée*, *plat* and *dessert*. I outline your story, as best I can. You become meal-time entertainment.

Where you used to live, there is no sound but birdsong. Someone has been mowing grass, and the air is sweet. The neighbourhood doorsteps are very clean.

It is perhaps for this reason that I notice, by the kerb, the compacted fluff of a vacuum cleaner. Your mother's defence against accusations of eavesdropping comes to mind – her assertion that she was not lurking by windows, but emptying household dust.

Was she?

The intimacy of this human detritus touches me. I think of your attempts to escape into a domestic haven – going about the little business of life as if nothing were the matter, with nowhere to put your pain.

It's a few minutes' walk from your old home to the *Préfecture*.

The *Tricolore* still hangs above the gateway. The *Préfecture* itself is bright with new paint. A plaque commemorates Jean Moulin.

At the corner of rue Saint-Même, where you ran towards

that lens, a café serves crêpes accompanied by little enamel bowls of cider.

We move up the street to where a shot was taken of you and your mother from behind. The camera's eye caught both the clamouring crowd and the familial skull shape, highlighting your mother's ropey trapezius; a cruel reveal of her aged body – and of what yours might have become, had you lived.

'Wait,' I tell my companion, feeling none of your suffering.

We stand, stupidly, in melted-butter sunshine.

I let down my hair, thinking to cover your nakedness.

Then tuck my hair into my collar, offended by my ridiculousness.

My discomfort increases, as we approach the site of that famous shot.

I imagine Capa crouching, watching your suffering through his lens, waiting for the moment when all the horror would come together beautifully, for viewers – myself included – who would find aesthetic pleasure in your pain.

Is that what I'm doing?

Standing where you stood, I look, attempting to see what you saw.

The cathedral looms. Gazing from a stone baldaquin is the Virgin Mother and Child.

I had planned to write you a message in chalk, or drop a flower.

Instead I stand in silence, listening.

A car door slams. A man asks his phone, '*When*, tonight?' A child wails for a crêpe with Nutella.

I am here, and you are still somewhere else, alone with your suffering.

It is this thought that moves my hand, later, in the cathedral. Standing beneath the stained glass, in puddles of ruby, sapphire and emerald light, I pick a votive candle: red.

I place it in the middle of the stand, apart from the others, light the wick, and say a few words that go up in smoke.

Juliette

You knew the lads on the metro were trouble. Double-hooded by their low brows and baggy sportswear, they seemed to lie in wait. As soon as you stepped into the carriage, their eyes singled you out. They shared an elbow nudge that was clearly more than camaraderie. It was no coincidence that they got off at your stop. But what the police agent wants to know is why you took the shortcut down the tunnel marked 'no exit'.

You hold the agent's pale-grey stare, seeking a clue to the words you should use. Your friend Justine would say, 'There's no law against it.' Your friend Sophie would say, 'Rules are just things made up by people; they don't have to be followed.'

'It's easier,' you say. 'There's no crowd to reckon with.'

'Why take the shortcut, when you *knew* you were being fol-lowed?'

You had felt a stubborn determination not to be intimidat-ed.

'Spirit of contradiction,' is the spin you put on this. 'I'm not much of a joiner.'

'Why go to a secluded place with two men, two strangers?'

It's true, the gut punch had felt inevitable. The bag snatch and phone theft too.

'Were you physically harmed?'

Bruises bloom beneath your skin, but you shake a 'no'. You don't know how to say, without sounding silly, that what hurt most is that they gutted your bag, found your favourite lipstick and, before running off, smeared it all over your face.

'We'll take a statement for theft,' says the agent, sliding your ID to the edge of the table. For a moment, he studies it poker-faced, holding it close like a winning card. 'You go by "Juliette",' he says, nodding. He hands the card to a colleague. 'Run a check?' he says.

The only explanation you can think of is that he takes you for a sex worker.

You straighten your back until you are literally looking down your nose, and give the lowdown on your name: 'It means youthful. It's a feminine form derived from the Latin Julius, a Roman family name that may be derived from *lulus*, the first downy beard-hair on a young man's chin.'

The agent's eyes thin to slits.

He calls you *grande gueule* – mouthy, then adds, 'For a woman.'

*

In your favourite café-brasserie, you are settled with your friends Sophie and Justine in your usual stall. Sophie's workday up-do is down, Justine's cropped hair is loosened into ruffles. An overhead lamp encloses you in a warm, tangerine glow that transforms the table top into a private beach or sandbar, complete with miniature paper parasols. The cocktails are improbable lagoons of swimming-pool blue, chlorophyll green and highlighter pink. A windowpane baffles the blare of the Paris night, so there is only soft music, chatter and the wet clink of ice cubes.

Yet your lizard brain still emits this quiet but insistent pip-pip-pip of panic.

Sophie's eyes are brimming after your announcement that you intend to go back to school.

'This is it: the beginning of your story!' she says.

Justine facepalms.

'I *knew* the business in the metro was an inciting incident,' Sophie protests, nodding fast, eyes wide. 'I told Juliette: things happen for a *reason*. I said, imagine you are the heroine of this story. Ask yourself: why did this happen now, to me? What am I meant to *do* with this?'

She had delivered these, and other Sophie-ish wisdoms, when she met you at the police station, along with a lumpy tote of 'first aid' – biscuits, unsold stock from the bookshop where she works, and an exotic fruit that she couldn't name. You had raised one eyebrow in disbelief. But now Justine's doing just that, you want to protect Sophie. From *maternelle* to *lycée*, you and she hid behind stories from the horrors of the playground. At uni she grew distant for a while – adjustment to many things, not least Justine, who got you into nonfiction. It would be just like Justine to point out that the 'inciting incident' has happened twice before.

Sophie turns from Justine, back to you.

'You'll be perfect for law,' she says. 'Bookish, scrappy. Can't go wrong!'

She said something similar when you switched from studying biology to art history.

'You'll be by far the oldest in class,' says Justine. Glancing at your pink heels she adds, 'It's a very conservative field.'

You think of your father, so controlled even in his choice of tie. You see him exploding, yet again, through the bottleneck of his white collar.

'Why don't you test your plan?' says Justine. She suggests that you temp part-time at the firm where she's a paralegal. 'We could do with someone with your personality and skills,' she says, nodding in that determined way of hers. 'Come by tomorrow at twelve-thirty, and we'll see what we can sort out over lunch?'

You give a firm nod, but your mind is drifting. 'Someone like *me*,' you think.

Sophie catches your eye, and smiles.

You see, as you so often do, both the confident young woman she has become, today wearing a home-haircut fringe that looks better than it should, and the quirky pre-teen who introduced you to lipstick. She had this wonderful way of applying the colour, working it hard like a Crayola crayon, with a joyous disregard for keeping inside the lines. You were enchanted – and utterly seduced by the pigment and shine of her lip colour. So much so, that you kissed her. The kiss lasted forever, and not long enough, and when you pulled away, you were scared. But she pressed her finger gently to your newly coral mouth. 'Suits you,' she said. It filled you with the same fuzzy pink glow that warms you now from hair-tip to toe.

Maybe Sophes is right: maybe this *is* where you start coming into your own.

You raise the Day-Glo liquid in your glass.

'To my best friends,' you say.

Sophie kisses you – always on the cheek, except for that one time.

'I'll send links,' Justine says. 'So you can prep.'

*

You wake, blonde hair pillow-tousled, blue eyes mascara-smudged. You fumble your phone to your face, check the time, and deactivate the alarm set to sound in seven minutes. It's three steps from fold-away bed, to bathroom, to toilet – small mercies of the city. With your mind still cottony from sleep, you settle on the seat, but before you've finished relieving yourself, your head has started serving up pep talk.

'Ask and the universe will give' – a favourite phrase of Sophie's.

'Dress for the job you want' – that's Justine.

'Don't fuck up' – your sister.

'I love you, no matter what' – Mom.

From your father: silence. Heart-crushing silence.

Hang on. You've strayed off topic. *Concentrate*.

Here's what you'll do: find a café near Justine's office. Read up, ready for lunch. Get some study in if you have time. Then at twenty-five past twelve – no, make that twenty – you'll go to the appointment. That's a plan.

You snatch a bouquet of toilet paper, wipe, flush and stand, ready to pay your debt to the gods of cleanse, tone and moisturise.

Take the time to love your face – another thing Sophie says. You're getting quite good at it, you reflect, as you shake floral dew from the expensive cleanser that was a pay-day gift to yourself. For the time it takes to sweep your T-zone with sweetly scented ointment, you just *are*. Then, you run a red nail the length of your stubbled jaw, wondering how the lighting is in Justine's office.

You don't have to pass. Sophie's voice again; something she said when you were new to heels, studiously wearing them morning and evening, trying to perfect the walk. 'There's no right way to look or move. No test.' She's right. In some better place.

Justine's advice comes to you: 'If you want to develop your career as a woman, depilate.'

You get out your razor. The one with the pink handle, for your face.

The black, multi-action, triple-blade, power-guard shaver is for your body. Your sister tipped you off that they do knobbly bits better – and cheaper. 'Don't buy the marketing crap,' she said. 'It's another way to screw women.' You haven't found a way to tell her how much laser treatment will cost.

You shave, stroking slow round lips and chin. Down-strokes, up-strokes.

Take the time to –

Nope. Even Sophes can't turn this into self-love. It's more like a ransom to be paid for your true self, daily. You work the blade over neck, chest, forearms, and hands, using your man's razor to make more of a woman of yourself. Each razor-stroke frees a strip of peaches-and-cream skin.

A quick pat of moisturiser – worrying less about taking time to love your face now, because the clock's ticking and if you're not early, you feel late. A dab of pink colour corrector round the jaw, some medium coverage foundation, loose powder. 'Putting on my face' is what your mom, an American, says when she's making up. To you, it feels more like what Michelangelo said about freeing the figure from within the marble. Each stroke brings your face further into the light. The techniques are more painterly than sculptural though: you work tint, tone and contrast; chiaroscuro for relief and depth, brown pigment to make the blue of your irises sing. The result is a made-up face, but it's yours, nevertheless – you made it.

You'd run with that power, if you could: eyes worked with iridescent shadow till your every blink becomes the beat of a disco butterfly, nails painted bird-of-paradise colours, lips slicked with an orange-red gloss like PVC...

But lunch is a work thing; it has to be lips *or* eyes. So nude-look lips it is.

You press a kiss on to a tissue to blot, then take in the gouged pigments and bright-tipped brushes littering the bathroom shelf. No time to tidy, you decide. This is progress; not so long ago, your every furtive make-up purchase was thrown away double-bagged to hide the shame, even from sanitation workers.

You turn, slip a hand beneath your breast, gently cupping it out of its box. Some days, you expect a higher authority to stop and ask for your permit. Mostly, though, you feel a blessed hush, as if cradling a sleeping newborn. The softness of the silicone skin still takes your breath away. You spray adhesive, apply, smooth on, remove for better adherence, spray, and re-apply till your breasts are double-bonded to your skin. You give them a stroke, squint at your reflection, mentally conjure up the pair that will one day live full-time on your chest.

You dress, opting for a shortish skirt that leaves your legs free to move, a bold striped jacket and lacquered pumps – professional but pretty. You fix gold on ear lobes and wrists, grab your laptop, sling your purse over your shoulder.

'Ready?' you ask the mirror.

*

You step off the underground train at your stop, feeling fully yourself. Lunch went well! A crowd cheers. The square above ground is a gathering place for activists and protesters of all kinds – there are demonstrations every other week – so you know the cheering is not for you. But it feels like it could be: you have a new job, which suits you from the flat soles of your pumps to the flick of your fringe. Everything's coming together.

Sophie said it would.

Halfway up the stairs to the exit, you see the crowd: a minority, multiplied. Your colours are suddenly wrong; you are much too white. And everyone else is wrapped in the colours of a flag you don't recognise – some North African home-country, you think, before reminding yourself that this, too, must be their home.

Our home.

Your home.

Only you can't get up the steps for the crowd.

You stand halfway out of the underground station, halfway in. A one-step no-man's land.

There are shouts for freedom, democracy, and something else – or maybe the same things, in a language you don't speak. A chant spreads through the mass. The crowd throbs like a great single-celled organism. The language barrier is palpable, forming a skin-like layer that you cannot penetrate.

The nature of the crowd – any crowd – becomes something else, on the edges. You read the body language of stragglers skirting the mass: their arms at angles, as if they're so muscle-packed they can't hang straight, legs too wide apart, caps pulled low. They shout '*Liberté!*' in time with the rest of the pack, but their place at the edge shows that they are not truly part of it.

You're not one for crowds yourself, but this does nothing to allay the fizzling sensation in your sacrum.

Some of the protesters on the edge peel away from the throng, to form a smaller group – one turned back-to-the-mass, towards you.

You are loosely encircled.

Above and all around: a panorama of coarse beards, black buzz-cut hair, bristles, biceps, trouser bulges. You scrabble for mental support – Mom, Sophie, Justine, your sister. You think of your father too, but block that thought. Your mind fills the void, serving up a random fact garnered from your short-lived biology studies: the species most like you is the one most likely to seek to destroy you, and take your place. That's the trouble with outsiders, you think – the danger; they can work like border patrol, attempting to secure a position in the order that excludes them, by pushing you out.

Adrenalin sparks in your kidneys, jags up your spine.

'Excuse me, can I pass?' you almost ask, but don't.

You won't. Why should you? This is your home.

A young woman appears behind you – one of their own, judging on looks.

'Come, you'll be safe,' she says, tugging you down the steps, back into the underground station.

You shrug her off, head back upstairs to the exit.

'I'll get help,' she says, and you are alone again.

As you emerge at the top of the steps, a crowd surrounds you. You scan for a gap, a weak spot, but find none. Beyond the crowd, too far away to be of any assistance, you spy the white vans and blue berets of the forces of order.

'Hey, sweetie. Hey, sugar,' says a puffed chest.

'You're a cupcake I'd like to bite,' says a pair of gym-worked shoulders.

'You were my favourite kind of boy in prison,' says a knife-scarred cheek.

You've heard it all before, or stuff much like it.

You make a move to go on your way, but a fist juts into your face. A rough hand rakes your hair, grabs a handful, and shakes your head like it doesn't belong to you.

You call out.

The crowd stirs. The backs of a few heads become faces that stare, then turn away.

Another hand lunges towards you, gropes your left breast. The adhesive rips, leaving you lopsided.

You don't know if it's the assault or the placid still-chanting crowd that riles you most, but you raise a fist, only for five to punch back. You fall. A kick shifts you up and a metre over. You land on gravel-grated knees. A fly is unzipped. In your face: the eye of a smug fat cock. Spittle. Laughter.

'Here it comes,' you think, tensed to the core against whatever 'it' might be – so much so that when help arrives, you flinch.

Underground-rail security staff blow whistles, part bodies. A pair of strong, uniformed arms heaves you up from the ground. You remember your father once doing the same when you fell from your bike; his rough, warm hands brushing better your gravel-pocked knees.

'This way, sir,' says the security agent.

Back inside, he gives you tea. He no doubt thinks he is being kind when he says, 'Exercise due caution in future, please, sir. Why go out dressed like a provocation?'

You look into your tea, examine its murky depths. You see yourself as you were moments ago: struggling to grab your bag, scuffed knuckles and fingertips scrabbling between boots and sneakers, trying to reclaim your scattered belongings. You messed up then, when you were splayed across the paving slabs – you realise this now. Not because they got you on your knees. No, you fell lower than that when you thought – just for a second, it's true – but you did think, 'This is not *our* way. This is *their* way. This is the way of the land *they* are from.' One more mental step and you would have sent them 'back home'.

If you look shaken, it is also because of this: they almost had you. You almost lost sight of yourself.

Mom helps you home. She keeps looking at you, her eyes all tender enquiry.

'I'm fine,' you say.

Her gaze only intensifies. She cups your face and holds it, as if wondering where she might keep it, which high shelf or cupboard.

'Really,' you say. 'All I want is peace, quiet. Please.'

When at last she goes, you lock the door. You max up the halogen till the ceiling is floodlit, then you crash, dead to the world, beneath the cold white light.

Your phone quakes. You do not pick up.

By morning, the quaking has become banging – Sophie's voice behind the door says open, she needs to show you something.

You open. Sophie takes your hands in hers and looks at you too long, reading each of your features in turn. 'Why this?' she says, teary, shaking her head. 'Why you?' She raises a hand to your cheek, but you pull away.

'I'm fine.'

She makes camomile tea. Handing you a cup, she says, 'You know it's gone viral?'

'What has?'

'Someone in the crowd was filming.' She places her phone in your hands, brings up a video, presses 'play'.

You understand no better as you watch a blonde in a shortish skirt and striped jacket climb the stairs to the metro exit. Then you *do* understand – you *know* what happens next – and your blood runs slow and cold, but you keep watching. Again and again this Thumbelina inside the phone tries to make her way up some steps, only to finish each time on the floor, behind a flurry of fists. Though she raises her chin to protest, stamps, throws a punch, the same thing happens over and over. And no matter how many times you see the video, you feel no less estranged by it. It *must* be you though; when the woman is helped up, you find yourself checking her fringe.

'What will you do?' says Sophie, taking back her phone.

'I reported it. Now I want to forget it. I want everyone to forget.'

You pick up your phone. Besides unanswered calls from Sophie, Justine, your sister and Mom, there are messages from absolute strangers. They want statements, interviews.

'How did journalists get my number?'

Sophie shrugs, shakes her head.

'Do they know where I live?'

Sophie holds out empty hands.

You turn on the radio. Commentators talk of an unprovoked attack on a transgender woman as she exited the metro. The woman has no name: she is a 'what' not a 'who'.

You turn on the TV, and that blonde appears once more, making her way up the metro steps. From every corner of the room, journalists ask questions like those that came to you when you were scrabbling in the dirt. They want to know how such behaviour is possible in our free, modern nation. How a group of immigrant protesters can call *our* home *their* home, when *they* do not share *our* values.

'Maybe this is a chance to speak up?' says Sophie.

'About what?'

She looks at you too hard, as if the real you might be hiding behind the curtain of your face. You stare back. The silence between you grows into something tangible that bristles and strains. Sophie lowers her gaze. When she raises her head again, she won't look you in the eye.

'It is your right to do and say *nothing*, I suppose,' she says.

If Justine were talking you wouldn't worry, but Sophes talks 'rights' only when things are wrong.

'Sophes –'

'No, you're right. Quite right.' She gets her things together.

'Sophes –'

'Call me, if you need anything.' Her kiss on your cheek is hard and dry.

When she's gone, the world feels smaller, meaner. The empty room accuses you. The four walls blank you. The mirror avoids your gaze.

Why *me*? You didn't ask for any of this.

You reach for the phone, bring up Justine's number. She'll say something sensible like, 'The victim bears *no* responsibility.' Or even, 'Sophes was way out of line.' But as your thumb is poised to dial, you remember what Sophes said – about stuff happening at particular times, to particular people.

Why me?

That same question.

Only now, it's doing something different in your head.

*

Next time you see your face on screen, you are explaining to a news anchor that the actions of the few must not be confused with those of the many, nor be confused with their cause, nor with the colour of their flag – and certainly not with the colour of their skin. You plead against intolerance. Quite well, really, you think.

You look to your friends, who are gathered around a tablet, their faces illuminated by the backlight. 'So?'

Justine gives an unequivocal nod.

149

'Oh yes!' says Sophie. 'That was powerful!' There she is: your first love – the woman who first loved you, lipstick and all.

'I did feel back in my own skin, speaking those words,' you say. 'More like myself.'

Sophie nods, earnest, starry eyed. You wish, not for the first time, that you could share whatever vision she has of the world behind her rose-tinted glasses.

'Let's celebrate,' she says. 'Lunch?'

Before anyone can answer, your phone rings. The number flashes up as 'home', but over the past months, you have learnt to read it as 'Mom'.

'Juliette?'

At first you don't recognise the voice, which has never before called you by your name – not this name, anyway. When you do recognise it, you can't immediately respond. Part of you says you never will – not after everything said and done. But the best part of you is bigger than that. It says, 'Don't let anger push this away; it's what you have wanted and been waiting for, for so long.'

You close your eyes and let the moment fill with heartbeats. You stay within its embrace until you are ready to speak. Then you answer: 'Papa?'

'Wonders of the World Await You!'

That's what our poster promises punters this season. It shows the Cirque d'Hiver, all streamers and spotlights, and a starburst of horses, elephants, and performers, filling the night sky with sequins and glitter. As I circuit the main corridor, spraying clouds of Forest Glade to cover up the smell of dung, I see that poster ten times. The chemical air catches my nose and coats my throat, but it's that poster which makes me gag. Each sighting's a reminder that I'm good for nothing. 'You're setting the scene,' is what Uncle Marco says, but I'm no idiot. If I mattered at all, I'd be on that poster, pulling in the punters.

After the Forest Glade run, it's time to tweak the carpet – another job Uncle Marco invented for me. Every day of the season, at twenty minutes to call-to-post, I tug the runner straight in the main entrance. While I work, half my family watches from gold-framed posters. I get right down to it on my knees – no messing about. There's little point in being hoity-toity when Great-granny's peering down as 'Arenic sensation! Venus on horseback! The Great Irena!' There's Dad too. He died when I was three, but there he is, larger than life: 'Sampion, lion tamer extraordinaire'. Then there's Uncle Marco as Monsieur Loyal beneath a banner saying, 'Audacious! Prestigious! Phenomenal!'

I hear him in surround sound because I get his ringmaster voice booming inside my skull too, trying to make like carpet tweaking is audacious and prestigious. 'Health and SAFEty!' he says. 'Imagine if somebody slipped and fELL!'

The one upside of carpet tweaking is that it gives me a chance to peek through the glass doors of the entrance, and snatch glimpses of the glitter-free world outside: clothes made for lives spent sitting, shoes good only for pavements, bodies so long and limp it'd be hard to imagine them doing anything more gymnastic than a forward somersault... I'd stand and stare, if I could – I'd crush my nose against the glass, but I know to at least look like I'm keeping my distance. Great-granny says, 'You can't play to the audience if you're part of it.' The rule's meant to apply to everyone, even ushers. 'You're all onstage,' she says. 'Never forget!' And I'm not likely to, with her peering at me from her poster.

One thing I've discovered, though, is that sounds are sneaky. So long as my back's bent, and my eyes are on the carpet, and my hands are busy smoothing, no one gives me grief for listening in on the crowd queuing outside. I let my ear fall in with the whir and grind of the men, and the swirling ribbons of sound made by the women, and the popcorn-machine splutter of the kids. I keep whatever words I can catch, stashing them in a mind-pocket, to help me get through the next job. I don't need much; just enough to take me elsewhere. Today's treasures: 'organic tomatoes', 'cuts commute time' and 'lunch at my desk'.

Almost ten to.

Time to get Great-granny, to put her in position ready for her 'act'. Of all the jobs Uncle Marco's invented for me, this one's by far the worst. I almost got let off, because Great-granny can manage, mostly, she just needs help with the stairs – and she was having none of it to start with – none of me, rather. Then Uncle Marco said, 'You need an attendant – it'll look better,' and Great-granny raised her chin, which is as close as she ever gets to a nod. I can't be early or late – The Great Irena's lost none of her famous sense of timing – but since I'd rather not go at all, dragging myself to her dressing room feels like walking the wrong way down a wind tunnel.

At an unmarked door, I stop. It could be a store cupboard, but everyone knows it's not. The plain door is Great-granny's way of reminding us that her legend's so great, she needs no label. Before knocking, I should 'feel' the moment, but I only ever feel dread, itchy tights, and my usherette jacket pinching under my arms, so I count down looking at my watch. With every tick of the second hand, I wish for a way out.

Three: flood.

Two: fire.

One: something – anything? Please?

Time.

Not surprising, but always disappointing.

I knock once, twice. Go in. There she is, with her black shawl and black blouse: eyes straight ahead, hair straight back, back straight up.

Ready, of course.

No 'hello', no look. Not since I messed up a splits test six years ago, when I was eight. I still hadn't come good despite months of pancake stretches with Mum, so they got in this sports doctor. Great-granny was there, and so was Mum – sweating. Mum spoke to me with the same soft voice she'd used to say 'there, there' when one of the horses had to be put down. Holding my heel, she said, 'Toes to top, lift.' I remember my bones grinding, my tendons fraying, and Mum nearly cross-eyed with confusion and frustration. She once sprained her ankle onstage and kept her performance face, so when she winced I knew I'd failed, and badly. The doctor said stuff about spinal rotation, pelvises, side tilts, and ended by saying I was a freak: 'Her body's not made for it; she's perfectly ordinary.' Great-granny shot me a look that almost sent me flying, and then left without saying a word.

I still expect none.

Great-granny raises her chin, and I get myself behind her chair. 'Organic tomatoes,' I think – a better word than she could give me, anyway. She jerks her chin like she's flicking a bridle. I think, 'Cuts commute time,' and push off. By now there are punters milling about, and ushers swapping trays and relaying each other without a word, as if they communicated by rubbing shoulders. I try to look as smooth as they do, but carpet, chair and corridor come together as unhappily as Great-granny and me. The rubber tyres of the wheelchair fight the carpet, and the synthetic fibres of the carpet squeak in protest. As I shove the wheelchair forward, I think, 'Lunch at my desk, lunch at my desk, lunch at my desk.' I briefly try to imagine a path that might lead to a sitting-down desk job, but it's too much with the drag of the chair. With my mind-pocket emptied of words, I turn to maths.

I imagine I'm cutting ruler-straight sections through the twenty-sided polygon that is the Cirque d'Hiver. It's twenty sides for sure – I know because my tutor, Madame Bernard, has me do geometry based on its layout. 'To help you grasp the concepts,' she says. I think I'd be fine with plain maths, but I don't say, because Madame Bernard is right in a back-flip sort of way: maths helps me get a grip, by keeping my mind busy.

The rest of me moves like one of our blinkered ponies, pushing forward without knowing where I'm headed. Great-granny's 'act' depends on her looking like an audience member for most of the show, but she doesn't like to get too close ('you can't play to the audience if you're part of it'), so I'll stop somewhere in an aisle, and it'll be the main aisle to the best seats, because nothing less would suit The Great Irena. Great-granny usually feels right between A1 and B1, but the exact spot is something she senses, so I go in slow, and when she closes her eyes, to 'feel' time and place, I keep mine peeled for the signal – a right-hand raise.

Not easy, because as the last stragglers are guided to their places, the audience starts to hum and throb. When the lights dim, the audience gives off a wonderful collective hush, like a backwards dawn chorus – more magical than anything we could come up with. I always want to squeeze in next to the nearest audience member and be part of it, but I think of Mum saying, 'Don't forget: you're onstage too.' This is something she says nearly every day of the season. I never know if it's to tell me off or to be nice, but I yank back my shoulders, crank up my smile. *Concentrate.*

There it is – just two fingers, barely lifted. *She does it on purpose – always testing, the old witch.* I put on Great-granny's brakes – fighting the temptation to leave them off in the hope of causing an 'accident' – shift to where she could see me if she cared to look, and give a nod that's sort of a bow. She lifts her chin, which means I'm good to go.

'Never run,' is what Uncle Marco says. He says it about the lions, but something tells me it's the same for Great-granny. So I walk to the door that says 'artists only'. I go through, as quietly as I can (for some reason, I always half expect someone to stop me). Then I run to the other side of the arena, because one of the dancers did her ankle in, so they're short for the intro. I do my costume change as I go, wrestling off my usherette jacket, pulling my ponytail tighter, and cursing as I yank up my bustier to make sure everything's in. Every second, every

155

breath, every movement in that bustier reminds me that if I were a proper circus type, I'd have a smaller pair.

I try to clear my head, like Mum taught me, so I can '*be* my body'. Trouble is, the more I clear my head, the more it fills. What I've been learning with Madame Bernard swoops into my mind like a trapeze bar that I can't help grabbing, which is funny – '*ironique*', Madame Bernard would say – because Mum spent that long trying to teach me how to grab a bar for real, and I never could.

'This is the diameter of the circle that is the arena. We can calculate the diameter by multiplying the radius by two or by dividing its circumference by pi,' I think, and swing through the air on that thought. I leave sweat, sawdust and dung behind, and fly off to a big top of ideas. One thought swings me to another. I remember how I have to tell Madame Bernard about the arena being oval, and does pi work for ovals too? I remember Madame Bernard saying that I could carry on with studies beyond the *Brevet* school certificate because I'm average, which is impressive considering. I'm about to swing off on that thought, when the wonderful feeling of being lost in my head reminds me that I'm more used to feeling lost in my body, and I tumble to earth. Or at least, I fall in behind the scowling Sambici sisters, just as the last time-call signals that we're almost up.

On the other side of the curtain, there's hush, and that collective intake of air that always takes my breath away. I find myself inhaling too, though I should be getting a grip on my breathing, ready to go out.

Uncle Marco's voice starts up over the speakers: 'The stars,' he says. 'For centuries, they have inspired and guided us.' He starts small and gentle. If sounds are waves – and Madame Bernard says they are – these are the little ones that lap at your toes. Uncle Marco says you have to start gently because an audience has to be a bit comfortable before you can do anything with it. Last time he said this, he added, 'like the lions, elephants and horses,' forgetting he was talking to me, who can't go near anything on four legs – doctor's orders. My face swells up like a clown nose. 'A common allergic response,' is what the doctor said. '*La fille de Sampion?!* She might as well be allergic to her own skin!' is what Uncle Marco said to that, so when he remembered he was talking to me, he found an invisible speck on his jacket that needed urgent and attentive hand-dusting.

Uncle Marco comes in strong for the next bit: 'For YOU,' he says, 'the Santini of the Cirque d'Hiver have sought out the brightest stars of the CIRcus!' After that, there's a blurby bit: 'Eighty-five years of circus tradition… twenty-five prodigious artists… daredevil high-wire performers… the best bare-back riders that ever lived… ponderous elephants… comedy surprises to amuse and delight…' I only half listen. I know the words by heart and there's not one to match treats like 'cuts commute time'. I *do* lend half an ear, though, because when Uncle Marco crescendos ('WE are the illustrious Santini, and we bring you the STARS!') I'm pretty much on. Since I can't feel the moment, I clamp a smile to my face and when the Sambici girls go, I trot out too.

It feels like dancing into prison.

The spotlight cuts off everything – even escape routes in your head. You're trapped inside walls of light, and not even word-treasures or maths will save you. It's just you, your hefty chest, and your two left feet, exposed for what you are. Everything in me wants to run offstage, but my own legs don't belong to me – not with Great-granny somewhere between A1 and B1 – so all I can do is shuffle-hop-step, while the Sambici sisters show the world how it *should* be done. 'It's in your blood,' Mum says in my head, but the only move that comes naturally is my lips moving as I count time and talk my way through: 'One-two, one-two, heel-toe-heel-toe-shuffle ball change…'

When Dan's hand breaks through the wall of light to start on the set change, I want to grab it and kiss it. Another one-two, one-two, and I'm back to relative safety behind the curtain, where I stay because Mum's on next. I see her as I come off. I wouldn't mind a hug, but I know not to ask. I get a look, nothing more – not even a smile – because she's 'in the zone'. Can't say I know what that means, but I understand that before a performance, Mum goes somewhere I can't follow.

When the music gets slinky, Mum squares up to the curtain. She stands eyes closed, legs tensed, bum cheeks tight, and takes a breath like she's about to dive into water, which turns her torso into an upside-down isosceles. Then she exhales, opens her eyes, and steps out with one perfect point slicing through the air. Uncle Marco's voice booms: 'The celebrated artiste Natalia Santini and her high-wire hoop chorEOgraphy!'

Mum goes out – all four foot eight of her – with the confidence of a big cat. Not one of ours. Not some hand-reared misery. Come to think of it, she's more like a lion tamer, perhaps. Maybe that's what she and Dad had in common? With each step, she claims the arena, controlling everything, easily. Even the sequins on her body stocking constellate to cover just what she needs them to, which gets me yanking up my bustier again. Her show's a bit sexy, but she tones it down for the matinée, dosing out enough to wake up the dads, but not so much that the mums are on the edge of their seats.

As she turns, swivels, drops, balances, I can't help wondering, 'How did that body produce something as clumsy as me?' One of the Sambici whispers, 'Neat single-knee hang,' and I remember that I'm meant to be checking Mum's timing, mining her moves for tips and ideas, assessing the fit of her costume… But then I drift off again. Mum's performance is so good that she stops being Mum after a while, and becomes her performance. I stop being me too. I stop wondering if I'm adopted, and give myself up to the flow of her body through space. Even though I've seen her act a hundred times, when the sizzle of a tambourine announces the end, I want to put my hands together.

The applause is still crackling as Mum comes offstage. 'Neat single-knee hang,' I whisper to her – a little lie, but worth it for the cheek stroke.

Alberto's up next. I watch, but only because I haven't got any homework and it's too early for the next Forest Glade run. Alberto goes in like a dummy, 'dropping' cups he's 'trying' to juggle. The audience laughs at first but soon they're gnawing their fingernails, slapping their foreheads, and clapping hands over their mouths to cap their 'oh, no!'s. Alberto makes like he's going to have one last shot. The audience sucks in every sound-wave in the place, a drumroll fills the vacuum, then he throws the cups: one, two, three, four, five, six – and catches every one. It's a cheap trick. Alberto says, 'I play with the fear of being an outsider. *I* am the outsider.' But he was born to perform. Even offstage, he shows off by catching matches with his teeth. When he's drunk, he catches flaming matches with his teeth. He's no outsider.

As Alberto's oompah music starts up, the dancers multiply, falling into place with each other like so many parts of a whole, then they clip-clop past in their top hats and tap shoes for the next choreography.

I set off alone for the last Forest Glade run.

The corridor's empty – not even a lone loo visitor to be seen. It's just me, my can of air freshener, and framed audacious, prestigious family members – and that stupid poster promising wonders ten times over. As I circuit the Cirque d'Hiver, my windpipe chalky with chemical air, I hear Uncle Marco's voice – on loudspeaker, even in my head – saying, 'No point in us taking the punters to the stARS to have them land in SHIT on the way OUT!' I think about shit and stars, and whether there might not be something in between. The ticket booth comes to mind and that's where I go next. 'Tallying up takings,' is what I'll say if anyone asks, but they don't. There's no one *to* ask because everyone's busy till the finale, except me.

I think of Mum saying, 'Don't forget: you're onstage too,' because I'm not. I think of Alberto saying, 'I am the outsider,' because he's not. The thought '*I* am' comes at me, but I pretend not to have noticed, because I don't know where it could take me. I try to cobble together something more manageable with polygons, pi, 'organic tomatoes', 'cuts commute time', and 'lunch at my desk', and I do well – get quite lost wandering in and out of imaginary lives beyond the glass bubble of the booth. I think of the doctor saying 'ordinary' and Madame Bernard saying 'average' and I get to wondering if I might find something for me out there. I sit up to take a proper look about, but see that stupid poster again – and only then think, 'Time!'

Five to finale.

I leg it, wrenching on my usherette jacket. The crackle of applause is becoming clapping in time to the circus march, so I speed up and skid in behind Great-granny just as Uncle Marco strides to the front of the arena, hand held high, top hat held higher, his red-sleeved arm outstretched to present the Santini of the Cirque d'Hiver. Marco doesn't mention everyone because there are too many Sampion Santinis and Irena Santinis, but Mum gets a mention, as does Alberto, and the littlest Sampion Santini, who toddles onstage tugging a Falabella, already a better animal handler than I'll ever be.

Uncle Marco holds out hat and hand again for silence, before saying, 'A celebrated artiste in her own right. Wife of Sampion Santini, whose father bought the Cirque d'Hiver in 1924. Mother, GRANDmother, GREAT-grandmother of the circus. She's watched EVERY performance since 1976 and tonight's no exception. People: The Great IrENA!' The spotlight falls then, like a pedestal back-flipped down from the big top. All heads swivel towards Great-granny. There's a split-second of quiet as the audience does a double-take, then as one they realise that the little old lady in the aisle is The Great Irena. They break into applause just as Great-granny raises her hands, to catch the claps.

Alone in the shadow, neither clapping nor clapped, I let my ear fall in with the sound of the audience – at first, just to feel less lonely, but then because the applause laps at the soles of my feet, swills round my ankles. It seems to get under my skin – tingles up my legs, tickles my guts, prickles my palms. Something carried in the vibrations makes me want to join in. I look at Great-granny, who's handling the applause as if it were so many ponies circling the arena, nudging the audience with a nod to the right, flicking a look left in case that side slackens... Her eyes are everywhere, but on me.

And I don't know if it's despite or because of this, but my hands come together making a clap, like a rogue firecracker. Even I jump. Great-granny's performance face slips. She slaps it back, and I almost expect her to reach back to slap one on me too, but I realise then that there's nothing she can do: she's on-stage. And no matter what Mum says, I'm not. So I clap again, and keep on, till my palms sting and my wrists ache. One of 1,800 people, all splashing up a soundwave. We build a swell so strong, I feel I might float away on it – the current of the crowd might carry me right out the door. I imagine being spilt on to the streets with the other pedestrians, the big top replaced by buildings and a beautiful big grey sky. I take a deep breath of air that's all people, pavements, plants, pigeons and cars – and I imagine a last look back at the Cirque d'Hiver, where I see that poster.

'Wonders of the *world*,' I think. 'Not wrong. Not wrong.' They await me…

The Comet

'Ah, Marie, toujours belle!'

Louis the presenter strolls in late, just as I'm about to take my break. He removes the coffee cup from my hand, grasps my waist as if to waltz me round Hair & Make-up, then graces me with three kisses – left cheek, right cheek, left cheek. My heart splits open like an overripe pomegranate. I would serve it to him on a plate. Spoon it into his mouth.

Louis has someone in for his hair – a guy who wears a suit and calls himself a 'hair designer' – so I know Louis is after make-up, not hair. But in the warm sunshine of his attention, it feels like anything might happen.

'If I asked you to marry me,' says Louis, his eyes weighted with faux gravity, 'would you?'

Something inside me silently cries, 'Yes, oh yes!'

From the make-up mirror, my reflection darts me a judgemental glance. It is easy to lose track, get carried away, when winter weekdays are spent creating spectacles of summer-evening beach parties for Louis's new show. Framed by the pitiless lights, I see valleys raked from my nose to my mouth, my brow stratified, cheeks sunk to chalky hollows. Beside my reflection is the back of Louis's head, the strip of tender skin behind his ears, and his dark hair, soft and glossy as a foal's pelt. He must be nearing thirty. Over ten years younger than me. Which is a lot, in television. For a woman. I issue a mental reminder: 'When Louis says "*toujours belle*", he means "still" not "always".' Without this discipline, my mind would grab that word '*belle*' as if it were a golden ball.

'I'm not the marrying kind,' I say. 'Twice engaged, never married.'

'Heartbreaker!' Louis clasps both hands to the left side of his chest.

I attempt a *femme fatale* half-smile, but my memory heckles. I see the lifeblood returning to my first fiancé's paled young cheeks when I let him off the hook. And my second fiancé, a retired notary, asking me with steepled hands to think, really, at my age, was breaking things off at all reasonable?

The producer appears, looking like he's been flung out of a fist fight: sleeves roughly rolled, tie skewed, colour high.

'Listen up, Louis,' he says.

I make myself small, busy my hands.

Louis settles himself into a make-up chair and leans back, almost too far to be safe. 'I'm all ears,' he says, closing his eyes.

'Guest line-up's confirmed.'

'Told you they'd confirm.' His tone is playful, but the producer flushes crimson around the collar.

'This is *not* business as usual, Louis. Not a flagging artist the music labels want to flog, or some friend-of-a-friend actor.'

'Relax.' That voice. Warm honey, poured slowly.

'The director-general has friends in high places looking to boost party appeal.' The producer pauses to smoke, dragging on his cigarette as if to suck the life from it. 'I need you to step up to the challenge, Louis. They want the popular touch. Our guest is none the wiser, so you're playing solo. Keep it convivial, fun. Funny, if you can manage it.'

'Business as usual then.' Louis cracks one of his grins and throws me a wink that lands like a surprise bouquet.

I give a circumspect smile. Word is that Louis will be on early-evening light entertainment only long enough to cut his teeth, then on to prime time. The thought sears my heart.

The producer puffs a snort of laughter through his nostrils. As he makes for the door, Louis salutes him with a languorous hand-raise.

'Marie,' Louis says with a sigh of satisfaction, 'I'm all yours.'

The small white suns around the make-up mirrors seem to blaze brighter.

I adjust Louis's robe to better protect his shirt, and gently lift his head to fit the hairband. He remains loose-necked, eyes closed, smiling. That's his charm right there: that mix of confidence and vulnerability. My father was the same – never hesitated to entrust his short back and sides to be 'coiffed' by my puppy-fatted fingers, whereas Maman was always fearful for her roller-set curls.

I swab cleanser across Louis's brow and the bridge of his nose. He makes a noise so unselfconsciously sexual, it's almost innocent.

'You do that *so* well,' he says.

He does this on set. It's a killer technique. One candid compliment and guests open up like daisies in morning sun. With me, it's no different; I want to tell him my secrets, confide to him my whole self. Not just the artful performance which, on a good day, still gets called Mademoiselle. But also the woman who comes home alone at the end of the working day, unlocks the door half wishing to find someone there, and wonders, as she steps inside the empty room, whether having her own place is reward or punishment for her choices.

'I *know* you,' he'd say. 'I feel like I always have. And tonight,

I shall reveal to the world the wonder that is you.' It would feel like when my father used to throw me to the skies, calling me his golden girl – the swoop and thrill of it. Only without the fear – the almost certain knowledge – that one day I would be sidelined, like my mother, looking on.

I squeeze a milky swirl of Embryolisse on to the back of my hand, ready to smooth on as Louis's base.

'Crazy,' I think. *Crazy for Him*. That's the name of the show. I must be, though. At least a little. Not as bad as the batch of girls they bring in to give the set its poolside feel – they'd do anything to be one of the bathing beauties that halo Louis's head on set.

When Gainsbourg came on so drunk they needed last-minute heightened visuals to distract from his slurring, the producer asked for more topless girls. There was no shortage of volunteers, all the girls so keen to get noticed. I made up more breasts than faces that day. One girl, who'd never been on before, said, 'This is it: my ticket to the big time.' I found myself wondering what 'big time' could possibly be, for her. The extreme tenderness of her young pink flesh made my eyes sting with tears.

I anoint Louis with barrier cream, select his Pan-Cake tones and pat on a terracotta tan so that his own holds up under the lights. He is smooth-skinned, slender-jawed as a boy.

'There's little I can do for him,' I think, not without regret.

Another stern glance from the mirror; I've made up enough famous faces to know that you go nowhere by playing tail to someone else's comet: Ardant, Béart, Daho, Gainsbourg…

Quite a list.

Louis's hair designer comes to mind. I wonder how many famous heads he groomed before being engaged as part of Louis's retinue. How one goes about getting that recognition. Whether it was the salon franchise that swung it. Or the line of signature hair products. Then it comes to me: the hair designer is himself a comet.

Louis practises lines: '*Bon* soir, bon *soir!*'

In the gaps between words, I sponge Pan-Cake around his mouth and chin.

Two of the ten models I finished earlier poke their heads round the door.

'Can we have the frosted pink for a touch-up?' says one, who I think is called Mylène. She points to her still-perfect pout as evidence. I nod and they sidle up, making shy eyes at their reflections as they seek out the lipstick.

Louis's gaze swivels towards the girls.

'Let me?' says Mylène to her friend, a blonde with a cork-screw scrunch-dry that earlier gave my arm cramp. The blonde puckers up, and Mylène smears a new hoarfrost across her friend's rosebud mouth.

Louis takes in the scene, riveted. I feel a cold blast like when I put the bins out the back of Hair & Make-up.

'Eyes closed?' I say.

He looks the girls up, down, up, down. Only then does he close his eyes, pursing his lips and swallowing as if he's eaten something good.

*

When Louis has gone to trigger the summer-evening glow and disco lights on set, I stand before the mirrors, framed by now-superfluous lights. Staring into them, I see myself ten years back, stepping shaky-legged into sudden daylight after a D&C. On my way down the clinic steps, I stalled, so cut loose by the procedure that I couldn't go back to my *chambre de bonne*. I made my way to a corner café and, braving suspicious looks from paunchy regulars, claimed a table. There I sat, for a whole hour, sipping espresso slowly, feeling self-contained and entire, wonderfully alone beneath my skin.

Where was I?

'Coffee,' mouths my reflection from the make-up mirror, though it's nearly lunchtime. I reach for my cup, but the studio's runner pops his head round the door.

'You're wanted,' he says. 'Make-up. Dressing room one.'

The corridor is littered with shapely limbs, high young breasts and flashes of monokini – a strewn bouquet of models. They nod like flower heads in blasts gusting from cameramen and sound engineers. The air is so charged with the desire to please, I almost smell lightning. It's like the whiff of ozone from the hot metal rods of Maman's rollers before Father's visits. That niff of electrified dust and scorched hair. And Maman's sparky energy as she scoured her cheeks rouge and scrubbed at cracks in her rice-powdered skin.

Father would blaze in from Ireland, making grand promises. He once promised no less than the world at my fingertips in the form of the *Encyclopaedia Britannica*, which he was buying bit by bit. Sweeping me on to his knee, he opened a volume at random and selected an entry: 'comet'.

'See!' he said. 'You'll have the stars at your fingertips too.'

The collection got as far as Volume Six, CALEB–DAMASCI.

When Father's visits grew sparse, I took to browsing the alphabetical lists of places, faces, flora, fauna and phenomena. 'Comet' was the entry I most often returned to. I learnt that comets are composed of volatile ices, that their erratic apparitions were considered omens for good or ill, and that the word 'comet' derives from *komētēs*, ancient Greek for 'long-haired star'. This last fact puzzled me; if anything, I imagined a fiery short back and sides. That the tail was dust sounded right though. Maman turned grey when Father stopped coming. She took to standing too long at the window, gazing out at the sky, which she said we shared with my father. I gave up on books and turned more seriously to hair and make-up, practising on Maman when she'd let me, trying to bring out, with brush-strokes, something of her lost lustre.

That's what I do for each of these girls: try to bring out their individual glow. Seeing them with their fixed smiles and overly ready laughter, I want to tell them they can get by, make their own way. Maman managed, as do I.

Don't I?

At dressing room one, the producer is holding forth in the doorway, with a glass in one hand and a cigar in the other.

The runner skids up and ducks beneath the producer's arm, announcing, 'Make-up!'

'May I leave you in the good hands of our *maquilleuse*?' says the producer, without turning to introduce me. It is possible that he does not know or cannot remember my name – a thought I stop trying to swallow when he takes leave of a 'Madame Veil'.

Not *the* Madame Veil, surely? Louis doesn't have important guests – famous, yes, but not important. All the same, at the thought of meeting France's favourite politician, my lungs fill.

The producer turns, nods, makes way.

I step into the room and there she is: Madame Simone Veil.

She stands smaller than me by a good ten centimetres, but imposing, unapologetically age-thickened around waist and ankle, and steady on her block heels. I see her as she is here, now, with her trademark chignon impeccable and a dress that couldn't have been better chosen if she'd been through Wardrobe: a good strong green that won't pale under the lights. And

I see her as she appeared in the newspapers ten years back: unsmiling but luminous, alone at the lectern of the National Assembly, defending her bill to an audience of suits, ties and comb-overs.

Madame Veil wedges her files under her left arm and holds out her right in greeting. I fumble my kit on to the dressing table and wipe my hand before taking hers. As we shake, I can't help feeling that she must know – must sense our connection. My *petit drame* came after the reform so it was no harder than it had to be, thankfully. Without the reform, I might have been *fille-mère* like Maman – worse, since I was hardly a girl when it happened. Or stuck in the band-aid marriage proposed by my young lover, with a makeshift ring. Or part of the grim yearly harvest Madame Veil spoke of in her speech – the 300,000 obliged to sort themselves out illegally.

I grope for words, trying to rise to the occasion, but all that comes to mind is the word pronounced by my best friend when I confided about the D&C: 'selfish'. It hardly compares with the slurs Madame Veil suffered when presenting her bill, but I feel keenly the tender throb of it, like shame or regret. I would like to have more to show Madame Veil for her pains – more to show for my selfishness.

'I do hair too,' I say. 'Not just make-up.'

I take in the professional puff and sweep of Madame Veil's chignon, and a flush crawls up my neck.

'I won't touch your hair, Madame?'

She holds a hand to the back of her chignon, as if testing its temperature. Her eyes – which are even greener in real life – are too clever not to know that I could never do a better job. But I see genuine curiosity when she says, 'What do you think?'

'Magnificent, Madame!' I say, meaning not just her hair.

I set out my kit as if laying the table for an honoured guest:

new sponges, freshly cleaned brushes, tints and tones of colours that might suit.

'Where do you want me?' she says.

I gesture to the chair, then think better, grab a clean towel, lay it over the back of the seat and stroke it smooth.

Madame Veil sits, resplendent with the self-assured bulk of late middle age.

'Will it bother you if I work while you work?' she says.

I saw – see – a film of her from when I was young, twenty years back. She wears her 'work uniform' of Chanel suit and chignon, and smooths cement with a trowel, ceremonially laying the first stone for some official building or other.

'You've already got the hang of it, Madame!' a man's voice jokes, off camera.

'I did that, you know,' she says evenly in the film. 'I did that when I was deported, so I do it well. It was my job.'

I remember stunned silence after – a stunned silence that may well have been my own. But it was what happened next that most touched me: she lowered herself to pick up her handbag. Such a simple gesture, yet after her reference to Bobrek, it took on a humble grandeur.

'I'll work around you, Madame Veil,' I say.

'If it's like that,' she smiles, 'I'll keep my papers for later.'

'No, please –'

She looks me in the eye – green almonds, greengage plums.

'Really. It's nice to put my papers aside for five minutes.' Her voice is kindly, but firm.

I reach for cotton wool and cleanser but find myself observing the action, one step removed from my own body. I felt like this once before – only then it wasn't awe that set me at a distance: walking past a café, on my way to the clinic, my still-small waist and already-swollen bust were ogled by men propping up the bar. I felt a fraud, ogre-ish. Even the trusty wrap dress and heels I had worn for courage confounded my shame. It was a snippet remembered from Madame Veil's speech to the Assembly that gave me strength – the bit where she said no woman goes light-heartedly. That kept me moving forward along my chosen path – feeling no braver, but at least understood.

I steal a glance at Madame Veil, half expecting her to say that she remembers being there for me.

She catches my eye, smiles. But she sits too well composed, hands on the armrests, as if awaiting the attentions of a dentist.

I am reminded: it is my job to be there for *her*.

Even the loveliest women occupy the make-up chair with a look of hope, fear, or both; there's always a sensitive negotiation of space – a certain necessary distance. But never more so than now.

I apply Madame Veil's base without fitting a hairband, working in chary little dabs – the manual equivalent of tiptoes. Like consecrated ground, her coiffure imposes a distance of its own. With each stroke I think, and try not to think, about how Madame Veil's convoy, on arrival at Auschwitz and for reasons unknown, were saved the humiliation of having their heads shaved.

'Eyes closed please, Madame?' I speak gently, stressing the inflection that makes my words a question.

She closes them immediately, but opens them at the first opportunity.

I touch no more than I need to, and explain each gesture I make.

I am careful not to look at her left forearm, at the serial number tattoo.

Elle est toujours belle.

The power of it – this beauty that 'overpowered the death-camp torturers', as the papers famously put it – inspires as much as it intimidates. I hold my breath to steady my hand as I line her eyes, digging deep for all the precision I can muster, shading with painstaking little strokes.

Over and over, my mind returns to the story of the guard who singled out the young Simone for lighter treatment because of her looks. 'One degree less tilt to the set of those eyes, one jot less gradient to the jut of those cheekbones, and she'd most likely be dead,' I think – can't stop thinking. The horror, the absurdity of it. And I wonder at the gall of the girl, accepting the offer only when the same advantage was promised to her mother and sister – even then counting the consequences of her actions in lives saved.

Emotion pushes up wordless behind my breastbone until I have to say *something*.

'Your dress is a perfect colour for television. Just the right style for the show – though I love the suits you usually wear.'

Madame Veil smiles and asks where I'm from.

'I was born in the suburbs – Clamart, but I live in Paris now.'

'And your family?'

Madame Veil's past casts a singular light on the question.

Instead of volleying my usual quip about being twice engaged, I return to the moment when I first took in hand the matter of marriage and children. I see myself returning my young lover's copper ring, saying, 'I was late, not expecting.' Him inhaling slowly, eyes closed, blenched cheeks pinkening, as if I had given the kiss of life rather than a lie. I looked down to admire my newly naked ring finger, and found it circled with a greenish tinge. When my lover opened his eyes, I was rubbing hard, trying to remove the stain.

'There's just my mother.'

Madame Veil nods slowly.

Pushing up stubbornly, again comes the desire to have more to say for myself.

'I visit once a week, but I have my own place.'

My bravura deflates as I mentally revisit my apartment. I see the paintwork that's so worn no one wants to touch it, and the lonely six-floor climb to my floor. My room, with the newly fitted water closet that I keep impeccable, but which stands out like an anomaly; a space cut clean out of a place that was never intended to accommodate such a contraption. And my *œil-de-bœuf* window, which allows in irregular jets of air but never opens far enough to relieve the heat of the building – that musty, dusty heat, which builds up even in winter, and festers, lidded by the hot zinc roof. And I wonder what possessed me to announce this small kingdom, this mean reward for striving, to Madame Veil, of all people.

'Ah!' she says. 'Wonderful to have that independence.'

Her smile dulls the mirror's bulbs.

Smiling back, I feel a sort of sunrise inside – something of the heady pleasure that surged through me when I first held my door key. And the sensation of freedom, when I broke off each engagement. Heartbreak apart, it wasn't unlike seeing a familiar city from above; the place that only moments before had felt cramped, constricting, becoming a world of possibilities. Above all, I remember the distance imposed by that lie to my lover. How it seemed to set me apart in my own reality. My own space. The space I needed to make my decision. Alone.

I cannot say I am proud. Nor do I regret it. I am only grateful to Madame Veil for making my choice possible.

I sharpen the lip liner, sculpting a perfect cone.

Madame Veil observes with corner-eye glances.

'Just your lips to do now, Madame.'

'*Bien.*'

It feels like a test.

Of what, I cannot say, but I see my life at a turning point. Until now: a series of 'not this' choices. Before me: unchartered waters. No more suitors to save me – at least, I'm not counting on any; Louis's sham gallantry shines like the last lantern glow from the shore. But I have skills, experience…

'I'll follow your natural contour, Madame.'

'That's fine – I trust your judgement.'

I trace her cupid's bow, espousing the form very exactly. My hand traces true, a faithful disciple of nature. With minute strokes I apply dark coral red, to fill. I pluck a fresh white tissue, blot gently. Build the pigment once again, downstrokes, upstrokes. Blot once more. Fix.

With a critical eye, I challenge the whole, ask if I can do better, more. Only when I am fully assured that I cannot do I ask, 'How is that for you, Madame?'

A knock. From the other side of the door, the runner calls, 'Time!'

Madame Veil gives her reflection a cool, appraising stare.

She turns and gives a nod of approbation.

'Thank you,' she says, offering me her hand.

As we shake, I bob my head, with all the emotion of a curtsey.

'*Non, Madame,*' I say. '*C'est moi qui vous remercie.*'

*

By the time I can sneak into the studio to listen, the interview is nearing the end.

I have my kit with me, as an alibi. 'For touch-ups,' I'll say, if anyone questions my presence.

The set looks flimsier than usual, with its paper-thin partitions and paintwork one coat deep. The girls in bathing costumes – out of shot, thank goodness – are quite simply irrelevant.

Madame Veil sits poised, knees crossed under her generous skirts, hands folded on her lap. She casts a couple of glances at the cameras, either clocking positions or slightly nervous.

Louis does a double eyebrow raise at camera one and rubs his hands together.

'According to your husband,' Louis says, 'it's impossible to get you to say something you don't want to say, or to do something you don't want to do.'

At mention of 'Monsieur Simone Veil' – the only man I ever heard of with the good grace and humour to be known by his wife's name – I feel a shoulder tap of apprehension.

Madame Veil licks her lips and looks away, but so fleetingly, I cannot read her expression. Is she unsettled, disgusted, bored?

'Nevertheless,' says Louis, 'I'll ask you something to conclude.'

Not the slightest trace of moisture blisters through his make-up. Louis's shoulders are loose, a smile plays over his lips. And yet, I feel a twinge of panic.

Madame Veil sits serene.

'I've only ever seen you with a chignon,' he says.

Something pulls taut inside me.

Madame Veil's gaze remains fixed, sphinxy.

Louis gives a guileless shrug, casts calf-eyes at the camera.

I lock my sights on him.

'If I asked you' – he says, circling back – 'to undo your hair –'

Madame Veil's gaze slips, but quick as a blink she redirects it at Louis.

He's got this, I tell myself. It's calculated.

'– would you do it?'

Sound in the studio drains away, leaving a vacuum so tenuous I hardly dare breathe.

'Why of course!' she says. The words skitter out too close together, at a higher-than-normal pitch. Her tone is brisk though; it's not impossible that she's playing dare, raising the stakes.

My heart beats a *chamade*.

Madame Veil lowers her head, raises her hands.

Surrender.

As she loosens her hair, my heart, shoulders, everything sinks.

This will make incredible television.

This will make Louis's name.

But I'm here to learn how *she* made *hers* – Madame Veil, survivor of the Shoah, Madame Veil, jurist, Madame Veil, international stateswoman, Madame Veil... talking softly while extracting hairpin after hairpin, because some young pup wants to know what she looks like with her hair down.

Louis watches like the rest of us, mesmerised.

'Long hair is so much easier,' she says, holding his gaze.

His smile wavers.

'With short hair, I'd be obliged to see a hairdresser every day, it's not so easy –'

Louis remembers chivalry: 'Let me help?'

Barely pausing, Madame Veil deposits hairpins into his palm as if he were a decorative pot on her dressing table.

Her chignon unfurls, falling down her back.

She sits, hair loose as if she had just got out of bed.

We become trespassers in the *boudoir* of a *grande dame*.

Louis sits on the edge of his seat.

Madame Veil plumps her hair bigger – playing an old role expertly, despite being shockingly over-qualified.

The biggest mystery is this: she doesn't seem entirely displeased.

The interview is over. Louis proffers pleasantries and smooths his trousers, ready to stand. Crew members detach themselves from beneath booms, and unfold arms from behind cameras. Madame Veil nods as people take their leave.

I stare into the lights.

Stepping out of the glare, Madame Veil approaches.

'Thank you again,' she says.

I must look dazzled.

'For the make-up,' she says. 'I knew I was in good hands.'

At a loss for words, I raise a hand to my heart and bow my head.

Madame Veil gives a nod of recognition, a smile, and goes on her way.

I watch her go.

When there's nothing but empty space, I look on still, blinking away light spots. Almost all intelligent thought has been blasted from my mind. I am left with a single notion: one word, which I am not entirely sure I understand, but which nevertheless blazes across the darkness like a revelation: *komētēs*, meaning 'long-haired star'.

Acknowledgements

The stories in this collection present female protagonists inspired by representations of females sourced from other media.

'*Lapin à la Moutarde*' was written in response to a Les Dawson mother-in-law joke. The story required research into the 'gynaecological tourism' that French women resorted to in the post-war period, before the legalisation of contraception and abortion.

V, the protagonist of 'A Steal', emerged from a file of official documentation amassed in the course of an identity theft.

The hero of 'After Ever Happy' and her back-to-front narrative were inspired by the music video for Alt-J's 'Breezeblocks'. The story sought to honour a forebear who divorced an abusive spouse at a time when divorce was not an option. For 'After Ever Happy', the Francophone artist Valentine Fournier was commissioned to create a collage. She worked at one remove from the text through makeshift translations, shared orally. To identify the pivotal point in the narrative, she submitted the story to an audit: 'What happens? What happens next? And after that?' From a collection of anonymous photographs, she then sought the face that spoke her 'reading' of the hero. Around these elements she built her collage.

'*Young Girl with a Flower Basket*' reimagines Linda la bouquetière, the likely sitter for the painting by Picasso. It attempts to engage with the life stories not told, and the issues not addressed, by the artwork's title, tints and tones.

'In Conversation with Ana Mendieta' considers the artworks of Ana Mendieta, and the reception of the artist herself. Research began in 1996 as part of an art history undergraduate thesis. More than twenty years later the story came out, almost fully formed, in about sixteen minutes – remarkable, for a habitually slow writer.

The protagonist of 'Feeding is Forbidden' was inspired by Jane, from the *Tarzan* films featuring Maureen O'Sullivan and Johnny Weissmuller. The story drew energy from the mismatch between the role models presented in the films and the demands of contemporary city living.

'Women's Business' features a narrator built 'inside out' from medical imagery, and was inspired by tensions between the juxtaposition of artworks by Barbara Kruger and Berthe Morisot.

The protagonist of 'All Things Bright and Beautiful' was inspired by *blondinettes* in a religious-education poster seen in childhood – or perhaps imagined.

'Three Weddings' retells the story of Galatea, from the Pygmalion myth, drawing also on George Bernard Shaw's play *Pygmalion* and the musical *My Fair Lady*.

The protagonist of 'Compassion' was inspired by a porcelain-faced doll.

'*Lettre à Simone*' and its postscript were written in response to the photograph *Shaved Woman of Chartres* by Robert Capa. The story mixes actual ekphrasis with notional ekphrasis. Film images were reimagined, to be 'seen' by readers through wordcraft. In the postscript, the station was shifted closer to the war memorial, so readers did not have to 'walk' so far.

'Juliette' was inspired by a news report of the assault of a trans woman in France by members of an ethnic minority, and this writer's initial 'othering' reaction to the aggression ('That's not French behaviour').

'"Wonders of the World Await You!"' was inspired by circus performers at the Cirque d'Hiver, and posters advertising their performances.

'The Comet' was written in response to an infamous moment in French television history, when a presenter asked Simone Veil to let down her hair. The artist Esther Ferrer produced a sketch in relation to 'The Comet', showing what the title evoked for her. Sketch and story differ markedly by narrative, but share a visual motif through a focus on long hair, and a common theme of female-to-female legacy.

*

Various family members, friends, teachers, artistic enablers, workshoppers, ideal readers, editors and proofreaders helped these stories along. In particular, I am grateful to Alison MacLeod; Beatrice Lamwaka; Byddi Lee; Caz 'n' John; C.D.; Françoise Harvey; Janet Skeslien Charles; Jason D.; Jon McGregor; Julia Skorcz; Kate Noakes; Mands; O.D.M.; Omaya Nasser; P.C.; P.D.M.; Penina Francus; SJ Bradley; staff and students of the Manchester Writing School at Manchester Metropolitan University, especially Gregory Norminton, Livi Michael and Nicholas Royle; and Tom Vowler.

Special thanks to Tim Shearer, Zoë McLean and Zena Barrie at Confingo.

*